# The Price of Freedom

Enyale Frost

Published by Enyale Frost, 2021.

This is a work of fiction. Similarities to real people, places, or events are entirely coincidental.

THE PRICE OF FREEDOM

**First edition. November 13, 2021.**

Copyright © 2021 Enyale Frost.

ISBN: 979-8201474843

Written by Enyale Frost.

# Chapter 1

## Jailbreak

Dark and damp. That's what this cell is.

Erin sits on a bed of soft moss, her back against the bookcase. Tomes, both tattered and pristine, jut out from the shelves; those books that entertained her for hours on end while she sat in her prison all by her lonesome. A cockroach scuttles by her feet, antenna twitching, but she pays it no mind. It can sense hostility, and it will attack. Erin lacks the strength to deal with a bug her own size before meal-time.

No-one ever visits her in this dungeon except the goblins who deliver her food. Nasty, green things, they are, with bulging eyes and rotten teeth. They serve the King, a ferocious dragon who rules over the kingdom of Avarice with an iron fist. Rules over Erin's life—and always had since she was but an infant. For twenty years, that dragon lorded over her, keeping her locked up in this hellhole of a dungeon.

Erin's stomach growls. Her meal should be here soon.

A set of footsteps thump in the distance as faint mutterings float down the stone hallway. Erin bites her lip to keep herself from smirking. Speak of the devil and he shall appear, indeed.

The goblin pauses outside her cell. It towers over her, casting a shadow that stretches till the walls. It pinches the tray of food between its knobbly fingers, which it then slides under the barred door with a sneer. Flicking it, almost. The dented metal plate drags across the stone floor, clattering against jagged edges.

"Enjoy, princess." The goblin wipes its nose of dripping snot, its warty feet flopping as it hurries off. Erin stares at the tray. She has learned not to trust the bread and to suspect the soup. All that is safe here is the cheese and the glass of water, so that is all she consumes.

Erin nibbles on the cheese. This should satisfy her groaning belly for a while.

As she downs the water, slurping up every last drop, she hears another bout of footsteps. Not the goblins' characteristic plodding but a meeker pattering. She smiles, cheeks stuffed full of cheese in her cheeks. *He* is finally here: her sole associate in this hellhole.

A boy scurries to her door, whiskers twitching, a whip-like tail curled around his leg. Erin rises as the rat-boy, Elias, retrieves a key from the recesses of his tunic and sticks it into the keyhole. With a click, the giant padlock falls, and it lands with a dull thud on the carpet of moss below. Elias grunts as he pulls the door open, flinching at the creak of rusted bars.

Erin steps out, pumping her fists into the air, stretching. A grin spreads across her face. Ah, how good it feels to be free.

Elias stands to the side, rubbing his claws, his gaze cast to the ground. "Where are we headed now?"

She almost forgot he was there. Erin sizes him up. Scrawnier than the last time she had seen him. Sallow cheeks, a lack of muscle, thin limbs... Did Erin make a bad choice?

Well, no time to dwell on that now.

"Out," she says curtly. "We're leaving."

Elias nods, following Erin as she strides down the deserted corridor. For years, she stayed up at night, listening to the crunch of footsteps and working out the goblins' regular patrol routes. There are three different patrolmen, each with a distinct sound to their steps.

And here comes the heavy stomper.

Erin ducks behind a towering stack of barrels, and Elias huddles behind her. She peeks out from her hiding spot, eyes trained on a piercing glow shining in the darkness. A hulking goblin storms on by, the lantern in its hand shaking with every step. The flame flickers, and so do the ominous shadows upon the walls. Once the guard reaches the end of the long corridor, it will turn around and come back again, before heading back down the corridor.

They have only one chance.

"Now," Erin whispers. She runs with her head ducked, dashing past the corridor. Elias is right behind her, his furry feet soundless against the stone. She dives between several crates and then presses her back flush against the wall. Elias quickly joins her, huddling next to her shoulder.

Footsteps resonate once more, echoey and fast. Not the stomp of the bulky goblin this time but a flighty one instead. Erin knows this pattern. The goblin's steps will become faster and faster, then pausing for a second or so, before fading out. They have five seconds until it comes back.

Erin peeks out from behind the crate and into the next room: a storeroom of sorts. It is brimming with barrels, boxes, and all manner of containers, with a pile of trash lying in the centre of it. The speedy goblin is a dwarf compared to Stomper, flitting around the heap, lantern jiggling with every step.

"What do we do now?" Elias asks, his gnarled claws wrapped around her arm. Erin forcibly shrugs him off.

They cannot stay here forever. Sooner or later, one of the goblins will notice her absence. They have to act fast.

The small goblin glances around, grunting in satisfaction before darting down the corner, continuing its patrol. As soon as its back is turned, Erin makes her move. Elias squeaks in surprise, scampering after her as she dashes towards the pile of trash.

She wriggles past a fedora bent all out of shape, ducking under a banjo with a splintered neck and snapped strings. Elias squirms in after her, breathless, ears flat against his head.

"Why'd you do that?" Elias whispers. Erin ignores him. She is here to escape, not to entertain his questions. She presses a finger to her lips and shushes him just as the goblin yips, hopping back into their field of vision.

The goblin sniffs the air, ears perked up. Erin holds her breath. Elias tightens his grip.

However, the goblin does nothing more than to scratch its nose, then turns around and continues on its merry way. Relief washes over Erin as she digs her way through the junk like a blind mole tunneling through a mountain of trash. She crawls underneath an overhanging sock, carefully avoiding a shard of broken wine glass and tumbles through piles of dirty bandages.

Erin emerges on the other end, heart seizing for just a second when she spots the small goblin bounding away, prancing off behind the junk. She and Elias have a couple of seconds before it comes back. They need to move now.

Erin slides down the mountain of trash, stomach dropping with the fall. Pieces of rubbish claw roughly at her back, her tunic nearly caught on a rusty hook. Elias stumbles after her, squeaking as he does. The slide delivers them to the doorway of the final corridor: the last obstacle between them and freedom. The small goblin's distant footsteps are getting louder and louder.

At the very end of the corridor lies a crumbly spiral staircase: the only way out of this dungeon.

Unfortunately, that is also where the final goblin stands. One who barely makes any noise, one who ever so calmly walks with rhythmic steps. Being the Warden, it would likely have keen eyes. Keen eyes that can spot even the slightest of movements. Watching like a hawk.

Just as Erin is about to take her first step from out the pile of trash, the sudden boom of a raspy voice has her heart rate skyrocketing, pounding in her ears.

"What the—? She's gone!"

Erin makes a break for it. Elias cries out in surprise. The screeches of the smaller goblin echo in the chamber.

"Find her! She can't have gone far!"

Blood coursing through her ears drowns out the thundering footsteps. Ahead, the corridor is empty, but she knows that the Warden is right behind the corner, his presence shielded by the wall.

Bells ring and horns blare. Erin skids to a halt and she stares down the menace in the doorway. The grotesque creature wields a club in one hand; in its other, it carries a net with its grubby fingers. The goblin—or troll, she is not sure—wears a mask over its head with only two holes to see out of. The rest of it is black, completely obscuring its face.

"There they are!" one of the goblins cries.

"Erin!" Elias cries. "They're on to us!" Elias cries.

Erin throws furtive glances around. There must be another way out. There *has* to be!

"You kids think you can just leave whenever you want." The Warden's deep baritone voice bounces off the walls. Stomper and Flighty approach from behind, the former slobbering all over the floor. They tower over the two children; Erin and Elias barely reach their kneecaps.

"N-No, I... please forgive me!" Elias cries, dropping to his knees and holding his claws up in surrender.

How slavish. Erin turns her nose up in disgust. Why did she ever choose to make a pact with this pathetic rodent?

"You have a choice," the Warden says, club slapping against its palm. "You can either return to your cell quietly, or we're going to have to take you by force."

"I-I don't want to die!" Elias' fearful cries devolve into pitiful snivels. He clutches at the hem of Erin's skirt. "Please, Erin. Let's go back. It's not worth it."

Erin kicks at Elias, her heel catching his throat, and he sprawls to the ground. He chokes on his own saliva, sending him into a fit of violent coughs. The Warden chuckles.

"Internal discord is never the answer to a successful escape, my dear Princess," the Warden mocks. Erin turns to it, glare steely. "The Prince wishes to avoid death. Perhaps you should grant him that much."

Erin remains silent, eyes flicking from corner to corner. A strange something lies near the wall, equidistant from her and the Warden. Glinting in the dim torchlight of the dungeons.

"I give you three seconds," the Warden says. Erin distinctly hears the cracking of knuckles behind her. "One…"

It is now or never.

"Two…"

Erin stares down at Elias, who still grovels on his hands and knees, shaggy fur hanging over his eyes.

"Three! Time's u—"

Before the Warden can finish, Erin grabs Elias' arm and drags him to his feet. She makes for the tiny, barred vent on the wall, leaping over clumps of moss and weeds.

"No! Stop!" the Warden shouts.

Erin scoffs. Only a fool will obey.

Flighty lunges at them, gnarled fingers closing around thin air, where Elias' tail had been. Stomper makes for the grille, shaking the earth with each step.

A shadow of a web looms over them. Elias screams as Erin drags him through the holes of the grille, just big enough for them to slip through but far too small for their pursuers. Erin staggers in the dark, edging farther from the goblins and the squarish beams of light.

"We must leave."

Erin runs, making her way deeper into the vent. As much as she wanted to leave him, she cannot lose him just yet—he may still be useful later. They're still far from the end goal.

The duo travels in silence, save for the trample of their feet against the moss on the path.

Elias chuckles. "I... I thought I was going to die there." The echo of the vent only amplifies his unease. When Erin doesn't reply, he continues. "Will this take us out of the castle?"

Erin flinches at the screech of a bat but collects herself immediately. "I wouldn't know."

It is not like they have a choice. If this damp, narrow vent does lead them out of the castle, then they will be victorious in their daring escape.

Yet, should this vent deliver them straight into the jaws of danger, Erin would rather die than return to that dark, dank cell of hers.

ELIAS SNIFFS THE AIR. "I smell fish."

Erin smells nothing but the pungent stench of moss and death. They have to disturb the corpse of a rat-girl lying in the middle of the vent and the cloud of technicolour flies it attracts. Elias threw up at the side while Erin merely kicked the body away.

No rat-people, dead or alive, shall hinder her escape.

Ahead of her, Erin sees a light shining from below. As she gets closer to the grate, she can finally smell it: the wafting aroma of dory sizzling in the chef's pan. Her mouth waters. She may never have had dory before, but imagination is a powerful thing.

A string of gruff incoherent mumbling disrupts her train of thought. She peers through the bars, watching as trolls shamble about in the kitchen as they prepare the King's next meal. The kitchen buzzes with activity as trolls stir broth in cauldrons, dice onions and peel potatoes.

Erin's stomach grumbles.

"Are you hungry?" Elias whispers.

"No."

Erin scurries past the grate, plunging back into the darkness of the vent. After much twisting and turning, it leads them to another grille, opening into a hallway draped with a lavish carpet.

The coast is clear. With considerable force, Erin kicks the grille open, the would-be thud of the metal plate swallowed by the carpet. She sticks her head out and glances around, arm over her eyes to shield them from the blinding light of the chandelier. For a castle on high security, the guards seem pretty lax...

Even so, anyone would be suspicious of a metal grate lying where it should not. Before the goblins or guards come by and put two and two together. They have to move. Now.

Erin sticks to the walls, trying to make herself as small as possible. Even by the grey shadow of the curtain, the ominous glow of the chandeliers overhead make them stand out like an inkblot on parchment. They need cover and fast, in case any guards—

Elias pulls on Erin's sleeve, making her jump. His whiskers brush the back of her neck and send shivers down her spine. "Erin!"

Why must Elias scare her like that? She had already heard the guard before he did. The guard who is making its way towards them right now, and it may or may not turn down this very corridor they are in. If it does, then they will be in big trouble.

Nothing in this goddamn corridor would make a good hiding spot. Not the cream-coloured walls, nor the windows, nor the *translucent* curtains.

The clanking footsteps get louder. They have no time to lose. Is there any way that—

A thought occurs to Erin. There *is* a way.

Erin makes for the curtains, scrambling to climb it as fast as her legs can carry her. Elias scampers after her, confused whispers streaming from his mouth as he grabs a hold of the swaying cloth.

The smooth fabric is tough to scale. Erin almost slips once or twice, but the adrenaline in her veins is enough to keep her head in the game, to keep her muscles taut despite all the exhaustion. She pulls herself up the last leg of the cloth. At the top, she turns her head as much as she can, stretching her neck to gauge the distance between her and her destination.

It's doable. The jump is doable.

"Erin! No!" Elias cries. "It's too dange—"

Elias can stay behind and get caught if he wants.

Erin holds her breath and soars through the air. For a single instant, her body is weightless, sailing in an arc towards the chandelier. She wraps her arms around the golden frame, stifling a sharp squeak as she curls her body around it.

The chandelier then shakes again as Elias joins Erin. His eyes are squeezed shut; his limbs and tail wrapped around a golden arm.

A sudden grunting below them has Erin stiffening. She glances down, only to see the guard right under them. It yawns, a hand held up to its helmet, before training its gaze on the length of the corridor. Erin holds her breath. As long as it doesn't look up...

The guard spins on its heels and marches down the corridor. Erin lets out the breath and gingerly shifts so that she's sitting on the golden tendril of the chandelier. She watches as the guard pauses at the mouth of the corridor before turning and walking back.

Looks like it's here to stay. How bothersome.

Still, they need to find a way across somehow. Erin squares her shoulders. Only one way forward. She's going to either make it, just barely, or plunge to her imminent demise.

Erin kicks off from the chandelier, arms outstretched and reaching for the next dangling fixture. Her heart thuds deafeningly in her ribs, blood roaring in her ears till she comes to an abrupt halt. She gasps, the wind knocked out of her as the arm of the next chandelier hits her chest. She scrabbles at the fixture, desperate to keep herself upright.

When she steadies herself, her grip tight on the golden arm, she breathes a sigh of relief. Below her, the guard continues to patrol, none the wiser to the two fugitives up top.

Erin glances at the rest of the chandeliers, running along the ceiling in a straight line, equidistant to each other. If she moves swiftly when the guard's head is turned, she should be able to make it to the end of the hallway where the tapestries hanging from the walls can serve as cover.

Elias follows right behind her, little squeaks and gasps escaping with each successful leap. Once or twice, the guard looks up at the creaking of the chandelier, but Erin makes sure to hide herself in its cluster of its bulbs with every tell-tale sound.

Thankfully, they cross the chandeliers without trouble, reaching a new hallway running perpendicular to the present corridor. In this new hallway, there are no guards in sight, no enemies to escape from. Not yet, at least. All Erin has to do now is to find a way down.

When the guard's head is turned, Erin jumps from the final chandelier over to a tapestry. She slides down it as slowly and as quietly as she can, careful not to burn the skin off her palms, while keeping a close eye on the guard. The guard currently stands at the other end of the corridor, the back of its head to her. Now's her chance.

Erin lands lightly upon the woollen carpet. She darts behind the tapestry, worming her way through its dusty darkness. Elias squirms in beside her, grunting as he shifts the heavy fabric to make room.

The clanking of boots grows louder and louder. Clanking boots? Where are they coming from?

Erin jumps when she catches sight of a black shadow passing them by, through the new hallway not covered with carpet. She crouches behind a wall, her pulse jumping. What is she really expecting? Of course, there would be a guard patrolling this hallway as well.

A staircase lies just across its breadth and at its base, a lobby that looks suspiciously like the main hall. That should be where the front doors are and also their ticket out.

Unfortunately, they have to get past this new guard, this new adversary, another obstacle standing between them and freedom. This guard stands at least twenty times Erin's height, decked out in gleaming armour. It is not defenceless either, sheathed sword clinking against its chainmail leggings.

If they get caught now, the guard will alert its brethren and their plan will be foiled. Erin clenches her jaw. She cannot let that happen.

As they say, where there is a will, there is a way. She must devise a plan to avoid detection by the guards.

To her delight, tapestries cover the walls, stretching from the ceiling to the ground, and statues provide convenient hiding spots. If they stick to the shadows, they should be able to evade conflict altogether. All they have to do is to study the guard's patterns.

A squeak in her ear interrupts her thoughts. Erin whips her head around, opening her mouth to berate her companion when his words stop her in her tracks.

"S-Someone's coming!"

Indeed, Elias is not mistaken. At the end of the hallway in which they stand, another guard marches towards them, donning armour similar to the first. With no time to waste, Erin grabs Elias' arm and drags him towards a pillar.

She dives behind its cream base, heart racing. Elias' laboured breaths are hot in her ear as they press against each other. The boots' clanks grow in volume, till they are all that fills Erin's ears.

"You seen those kids?" a gruff voice asks—belonging to the guard they hid behind the pillar to avoid.

"If I did, I'd have hollered." The other guard's voice is significantly higher, bordering on squeals.

Erin frowns. The guards are searching, as she would expect them to be.

"Think they probably escaped by now?" the gruff guard asks.

"Maybe. But I do want that reward, though."

They continue talking, giving Erin and Elias the opportunity to slip from one pillar to the next, sheltered from the eyes of the guards. The escape felt like it would never end, but here they are, soon nearing the staircase. All the while, the guards are still engaged in trivial conversation.

A yawn snatches her attention. Erin hugs a pillar, trying to meld right into it, to become one with the cement structure. Beside her, Elias is equally tense, his shoulders hunched and breathing shallow.

Approaching their hiding spot from the corridor perpendicular is yet another guard, this one carrying a halberd. It walks stiffly, as if its knees are eternally locked. However, this guard is different. Unlike the others, its chainmail is splashed with an emblem: the emblem of the Captain of the Royal Guard. It stands at the mouth of the hallway, raising its fist at the slacking guards.

"Oi! Get back to work, you lazy assholes!"

The two guards jump, ceasing their small talk immediately. Erin lets out a shuddering breath as the Captain leaves. The other two return to their routine, the one striding quickly towards them grumbling under its breath, while its friend disappears behind the wall.

Erin bites her lip. They are so close but so far away. As long as the guards continue on their delegated routes, they are trapped. Is it possible to lure them away? Is there something that she can use to create a distraction?

Well, there *is* something. As much as Erin would prefer to save him for more dire situations...

Elias' head is turned, more concerned with the pacing guards. Erin brings her foot down on Elias' tail.

Elias shrieks, and Erin bolts.

"What was that?"

"Over there! There's a kid there!"

Erin would have found Elias' confused face so wonderfully cute if not for the gravity of the situation. "Erin? Erin! Wait!"

Erin ignores him. She clambers up the wooden pedestal by the stairs. Elias squeaks and scrambles up the pedestal after her. Erin grits her teeth. She hadn't expected Elias to follow so quickly. Now he'll lead the guards right to her!

The Captain makes a lunge for them, only to be met with a face full of water and roses. The vase atop the pedestal tumbles to the ground, reduced to nothing more than glittering shards, impossible to tell what it even looked like before. The Captain falls back, landing with a thud on its rear.

"Erin!"

Elias scrambles up the pedestal, claws affording him traction he needs on the varnished wood. "Why'd you—" Elias starts, breathless.

"For our escape. Come on."

Erin slides down the banister, heat building up under her feet as she rockets down to the foyer. Elias follows right after, pained winces and squeaks ripping from his throat.

At the end of the bannister, Erin takes a leap and lands on a velvet carpet. She skids to a halt when she notices the battalion of guards rushing out from the other end of the foyer. They head for the large double doors, effectively blocking their exit.

How dare they?

Elias grasps her arm, trembling in fear. "Where do we go now?"

Erin sniffs. A familiar smell permeates the air. The aroma of cooked fish, lemon, and spices. The kitchen must be nearby. Filled with chefs, with fire and water and all sorts of obstacles that may impede the guards' advances. With all other routes blocked by guards, she must take her chances.

"This way."

Erin darts below the stairs, out of view. She keeps her nose and ears peeled for the smell of the fish and the clang of armour.

"There they are!"

Shoot! They're spotted.

Erin heads in the direction of the smell, Elias close behind her. The clanking of the guards' boots increases in volume with each step. Upon reaching a grate in the wall, Erin grits her teeth, pulls it open, and rolls through. She ends up on the other side, behind a stove in the kitchen. Elias stumbles out after her.

The doors slam against the walls with two resounding bangs. Erin sticks to the shadows, pressing her back as flat as she possibly can against the warm stove as she watches the guards closely.

"Where are they?" the Captain shouts, storms from counter to counter, shoving hapless chefs aside. Appearing at the door are a legion of guards, a few of them edging uncertainly into the trolls' domain.

"The 'ell's goin' on 'ere?" The head chef waves a skillet at the Captain. "What're ya doin' back 'ere in my kitchen, eh?"

With the conflict between the troll and the Captain keeping them busy, it is time for Erin to make her move. There must be a way out from here.

All of a sudden, an idea occurs to her. A window would work—or a vent. Even a rubbish chute would suffice. The goblins always talked about being shoved down the chute as punishment. That will certainly give them a quick way out.

Erin creeps along the walls, hoping not to draw the attention of neither the trolls nor the guards. Each step is quiet and sure. Elias scampers behind her, clutching his tail between his paws.

"Yer eyes've gotta be deceivin' yer, ya twat," the head chef hisses. "Begone, 'e lot of ya!"

Erin ducks under another stove, Elias slotting himself beside her. Most of the trolls have returned to their stations to continue preparations for lunch. No breathing room left for the two fugitives.

"What do we do now?" Elias whispers.

Erin wishes he would just shut up.

Just then, a ding screeches to their right. Erin's heart leaps to her throat, head snapping to the source: an oven.

A troll waddles over, clad in an oily, stained apron. She opens the oven, pudgy hands grabbing the tray and dragging out the burned remains of what was probably a pie.

"Oh dear," she mutters under her breath.

Glancing around furtively, she removes her apron, draping it over the handle of the oven, and shambles off. Erin's gaze darts from one troll to the next, each occupied with their own task. Wasting no time, she sprints towards the apron. She lifts herself over and into the pocket, pinching her nose as she takes in the fumes of whatever had died in here.

Ah.

No wonder her landing had been exceptionally soft if not prickly.

She had just dropped into a pocket of dead rat-people. Most of them lacking heads, and some missing limbs. A few of them have tails bent at awkward angles, and some sport a coat of blood-matted fur. Erin glances up, if only to see Elias peering down at the graveyard of rat-people corpses, his jaw agape.

"No." Elias shakes his head. "I refuse. There must be another way, Erin."

"Do you want to escape or not?" Erin snarls.

"I want to, but..."

"Get in or get out." If Elias stays like that any longer, he could lead them right to her.

Elias chews on his lip, squeezing his eyes shut and tumbling in. Just in time too. Within seconds, the apron is lifted into the air, the sea of corpses shifting with each jerk. Elias whimpers, and Erin clamps a hand over his mouth.

The apron settles against something rotund. The troll's protruding belly, perhaps. Erin peeks out from the pocket, barely able to see just where they are headed.

"Brenda! Could'ja c'mere and git that pot and chuck it? Blemished, it is. Fucker added too much pepper."

A skip! Is that their ticket out?

The troll sighs, changing course and ambling towards said pot. Now, all Erin has to do is to devise a plan to get into the skip without getting spotted. Ideally, not by the Captain still in the kitchen, arguing pointlessly with the head chef.

Just then, the apron is lifted once more over Brenda's head. A splintered bone scratches Erin across the cheek, drawing blood. Elias reaches out to her, a claw poised in the air as thought it were waiting for a response. Erin pretends not to notice.

Brenda takes her apron off whenever she uses the rubbish chute, and Erin is stupid for not realising that she did just that earlier. The troll drapes the apron over another counter this time, the lower half of its apron now inches from the floor. It appears that they have been transported into an entirely new section that they have yet to explore.

The chute is probably somewhere here.

Brenda hobbles off, heading towards the island in the middle of the room. Erin watches from the pocket, fingers clenched around the edge of the fabric. Brenda grabs the pot from the stove and makes for the rubbish chute at the far end.

They must leave the apron before Brenda returns, or there may not be another chance. Erin climbs out, dropping to the ground. She winces, picking herself up and rubbing at her elbow.

All of a sudden, a shadow looms over her. When Erin looks up, she gasps at the crimson orbs staring down at her, floating within the shadowy abyss that is the face of the Captain. How did it find her?

"I thought I smelled a rat!" it exclaims.

The Captain lunges for her. Erin dives out of the way, rolling under a stove. Pandaemonium seizes the kitchen, with trolls shouting and the singing of blades ripped from their sheaths. Erin, however, is more concerned with the golden gauntlet reaching for her, its fingers outstretched.

"Erin! In here!" Elias yanks at her arm and drags her to a hole in the wall. It resembles one gnawed by a mouse, flakes of paint scattered along the dusty floor. Erin follows him through, into the wall, into a world of darkness. Elias guides her up a sloping plank, tunnelling through the wall.

The thin layer of wall next to them rumbles, and Elias yelps when a blade stabs through the plaster in front of them. Wisps of dark energy curls around it like smoke, the tendrils of black reaching for Erin like gnarled fingers. The blade retracts, now replaced with an angry eye peering in.

"I see you, rats!" the Captain yells.

"Go!" Erin shrieks. "Hurry!"

Elias scampers up the slope, keeping his claws firm around Erin's arm and tugging her along with him. The sword stabs through the wall behind them, where Erin had been just seconds prior. Together, the duo continues to run, deftly dodging each jam of the sword.

Very soon, Erin sees their goal: another hole in the plaster with bright light filtering through. It probably opens back up into the kitchen, and it must bring them closer to the skip. It has to!

Elias is the first to flee from the confines of the passageway, away from the jabs of the blade. Brenda stands with her foot on a metal pedal, pot of sludge in hand. Her back is turned to the open chute as she stares at, wide-eyed, at the sudden siege of the kitchen.

"Now see here, you cretins!" Brenda cries, finding her voice at last. "How dare you come in here and—"

The Captain ignores her and sprints towards Erin and Elias. Erin pulls herself up onto a weighing scale, knocking over a beaker. It shatters, covering the countertop with flour. Brenda screams and drops the pot, sludge spilling all over the tiles.

Erin ducks behind a bottle of oil which the Captain overturns with a sweep of its arm. The chute is within reach. Just a little more...

The Captain swings its sword, sending jars of condiments flying off the side. Brenda screams and jumps away from the chute, letting go of the pedal.

"No!" The scream that tears from Erin's throat is unlike anything she'd ever felt before. Right in front of her eyes, the chute swings close with a loud snap. It encompasses her shock, her desperation, her *despair*. Erin stares, wide-eyed, at the closed chute, which she would have reached in the next couple of seconds had it not slammed shut. For her plan to be foiled at this stage... Surely not!

"Erin!"

Elias overtakes her, furry feet carrying him faster and farther. He sprints towards the edge of the counter, now drawing the Captain's attention to him. What is he doing, that fool?

Elias makes a death-defying leap, and for a single instant, time slows. Elias sails through the air, grabbing onto the handle of the chute and pulling it open with his weight. The gap is not wide, but it is certainly big enough for Erin to slip on through.

Erin leaps into the pocket of metal. Now all Elias needs to do is to let go...

"Erin! Help me!" Elias cries. Erin can only imagine his struggle, the way he hangs from the handle, at the mercy of the rat-eating Brenda and the menacing Captain of the Guard. "Erin!"

Erin merely smiles.

That's one liability gone.

Erin meets Elias' gaze for a brief second as he is snatched up by Brenda's crushing grip. The betrayal in his eyes is delicious, something to be delightfully consumed.

"Goodbye, Elias," Erin whispers, more to herself than anyone else.

The pocket of the chute jerks and punts Erin into the darkness, away from Elias, away from the kitchen, and out into the big, wide world.

# Chapter 2

## Forest of Fairies

Head tucked, body tense, Erin tumbles from the chute into a heap of rubbish. A murder of crows squawks, flapping their wings and taking to the skies. A beetle scuttles on by.

A beetle of a size she can crush underfoot.

Erin coughs, trying her hardest to hold her breath and keep the putrid stench at bay. She hops to her feet, stumbling on shards of broken glass and splintered wood, stepping over puddles of cake, slabs of rotten meat, and cracked eggshells. She slides down the heap, wincing at the graze of rough logs and steel against the back of her thighs. As painful as that was, she's glad to leave the pile of filth behind her.

Feet tapping lightly on the ground, Erin finds herself at the mouth of a gravel road winding through the forest ahead. The blue glow of fireflies is magical against thick canopies, bright enough to illuminate the path but dim enough to lend mystery to the expanse that lies beyond the copse. Erin would have stayed to marvel at the sights if not for the echoing yells of enraged guards from within the castle.

No time to waste. She must run.

And the only way for her to go is through the mystical forest.

ERIN KEEPS TO THE GRASS for walking on the gravel would make too much noise. She can no longer hear the clinking armour of the guards, only the howl of wolves and the tinkling laughter of fairies.

Fireflies flit to and fro, surrounding her with their ethereal, sapphire luminescence.

Her stomach rumbles. How long has it been since she's trudged along this path—getting nowhere? A few minutes? Hours? An eternity? She should have snagged something from the kitchen when she had the chance.

A sudden rustle of leaves catches Erin's attention. She goes stock-still, glancing towards the sound.

The forest darkens. The blue around her vanishes, the fireflies frightened by a hostile presence. Erin glances about, gaze darting along the undergrowth, the bushes, and the trees. They flit to the owl perched on the woods, its knowing eyes seeing all. And then to the still leaves of the thicket.

Then, she sees *it*.

A pair of yellow eyes. Watching her. Leering.

Erin scarcely dares to breathe. Those beastly eyes exude ferocity, belonging to a creature at least ten times her size. Brandished fangs glint in the moonlight, and slobber dribbles from a gaping jaw. One that could probably rip her throat out without a second thought. There is nothing nearby she could use to defend herself. Not even a branch.

Then, the wolf pounces.

She screams, throwing herself into a patch of thistles. The wolf soars over her head, missing by a hair's breadth. The thorny plants scratch at her skin, jabbing painfully into her flesh. Erin coughs from the spray of dirt, ducking beneath blades of grass as the wolf leaps at the patch.

Erin stumbles through ensnaring leaves, caught in an unrelenting chase. The wolf's paws slam hard into the gravel, kicking pebbles and dirt into the air. Erin leaps over a large rock, rolling onto the grass and into a bush.

Erin shrieks as the wolf scatters the thick brush with a powerful swipe of its paw. Leaves and rose petals whip up around her like a storm, obscuring her view ahead. Most importantly, the destruction of the undergrowth leaves her without cover. Nowhere to run, nowhere to hide. The beast could gobble her up with a swift snap of her jaw.

The dense grass is not easy to run in either, not with her flowy tunic and baggy pants, not with gnarled knots of grass and snagging stems of hawthorn. With so many obstacles in Erin's way, it is only a matter of time before the inevitable...

Her toes dig into a jutting root. Her momentum jerks to a halt and she plants, face first, into the soil. She wheezes, her throat constricted. Her lungs are close to bursting, the muscles screaming for reprieve.

A shadow looms over Erin. She whips her head back, meeting the beast's triumphant glare with a fearful one. She barely has time to blink; a million thoughts race through her head before the beast goes flying.

Away from her, that is. It crashes into a tangle of roses; an agonised whine is drawn from its pitiful form.

Erin stares at the arrow lodged in the wolf's throat, no bigger than its snout. The beast's body spasms, paws twitching, guttural growls interrupted by heaving breaths. In a matter of moments, the wolf moves no more.

Erin's legs have lost all of their strength, her body frozen to the spot. A breeze washes over the forest, whistling through the leaves. She glances at the branches, the bushes, the boulders embedded in the soil. The fireflies return, lighting up the forest once more.

"Who are you?" Erin shouts. "Show yourself!"

A sudden thud draws Erin's gaze. The adrenaline picks up again, thrumming through her veins, keeping her light on her feet and ready to bolt at a moment's notice. She squints at the approaching hooded figure who is—thank goodness—her height. He is draped in dull cloths meant for a hunter, like the hunters told in Erin's stories. A figure carrying a bow in hand and a quiver of arrows on their back.

Did they shoot the arrow?

The blue fireflies surround the figure, as though they were paying homage to their saint. The figure then reveals a shock of golden hair and his face, the hood now pooling around his neck.

"Hey there." He speaks with a velveteen lilt, one that Erin would not expect from a man accustomed to the outdoors.

"Who are you?" Erin asks. He cannot hope to woo her with his handsomeness, pointed ears, and boyish grin. Again, not a face you would associate with a veteran of the wilderness.

"You can call me Karl," he says. "What's yours, princess?"

Erin flinches. "Don't call me that."

"I might if you won't give me your name."

Erin narrows her eyes, sizing him up. She's heard stories about the forest's inhabitants from the chatty goblins. They said it was extremely dangerous to give your name to the fairies, for one's name holds immense power.

And while he may have pointed ears and is certainly the size, Karl lacks the wings. Then again, he may be hiding them cleverly; Erin would not put it past him.

"Ellie," she finally says. "My name's Ellie."

"Ellie, huh?" Karl smiles, sauntering over to her. "It's a pretty name."

Karl extends a hand. Erin eyes it closely.

"I'm seriously not out to kill you if that's what you're concerned about," he says. "If I wanted to, I would have done it a long time ago."

"That's not what I'm worried about."

"I'm not going to hurt you either." Karl gestures at his ears. He turns around, showing Erin all sides of his body. "See? I've got nothing on me."

Apart from the bow and arrows. Erin narrows her eyes.

"Take off your shirt."

Karl stares, a most comedic expression on his face. He laughs, wrapping an arm around his middle.

"Are you crazy? No way."

Crazy? No, Erin is not crazy in the slightest. She folds her arms.

"How can I be sure that you're not lying?"

"What about you, then?" Karl challenges. "Do you have anything dangerous on you?"

Erin holds her hands above her head, meeting Karl's gaze with one just as intense. "You're free to search me if you wish."

Karl opens his mouth to speak then, only to be interrupted by a howl in the distance. Erin turns to the woods in search of the source, but there is none to be found. A shiver travels down her spine.

"It's not safe here," Karl says. "We should go back."

"Back? Where?" To his fairy kingdom, perhaps?

"My campsite."

Campsite? Why is he camping here of all places? She glances first at the darkened sky, barely visible through the thick brush, and then back at the wolf. This encounter is proof that she is unable to survive alone in these unforgiving woods; it's in her best interests to follow Karl. For now.

Karl notices her apprehension and extends a hand again.

"Come on. Let's go. It's not far from here."

Erin ignores the gesture and marches on. Karl chuckles, falling into step beside her, fingers clasped behind his head.

"It really hurts my feelings when you're so suspicious of me, you know?"

Does Erin care? Not particularly. They're no more than strangers, two people who met thanks to a wolf. Although if Karl can provide her a place to sleep and a bit of food, she would gladly accept his help. However, they will part ways just as soon as she wants them to.

Karl's campsite is in a tiny clearing surrounded by bushes and flowers. An overhang built from soil and grass, and topped with a tiny daisy, offers shelter from the elements. Cinders smoulder in a pit that used to be Karl's campfire. He tosses branches and twigs into the pile of charred logs before retrieving a small box.

Erin watches, enraptured, as Karl removes a thin, short stick and dashes its dull, red end across the side of the box. It ignites, the flame glowing ever brightly in the dark of the night.

"How did you do that?"

Karl tosses the burning stick into the pile and sets the logs alight. He watches her with an incredulous expression. "Have you never seen matches?"

Erin shakes her head, her gaze falling on the enchanting dance of fire. The warmth is enticing, and Erin holds her hands out like a moth drawn to the flame.

"Here."

Erin stares at the bread and cheese handed to her. Her stomach growls at the tasty sight, making the most gruesome sound. Karl waves it in front of her face.

"Hello? Earth to Ellie."

If one accepts food from the Fae, then they would never be able to leave their land. That's how the stories go, don't they? Or did that only apply to food taken from the forest? Erin is not sure if she is willing to take that risk.

"I'm seriously not out to get you. Serious. Cross my heart and hope to die." His tone lacks impatience and his smile, the malice. Perhaps he truly is friendly after all.

Erin takes the bread and inspects it. Nothing seems out of the ordinary. It looks just like what she would have had as a meal back in the dungeons. Except that this slice is not stale. Not in the slightest. The cheese is stunningly yellow as well, without the blue dots of mould she was accustomed to.

She bites into the crispy crust, savouring the taste of the bread alone. Complementing the next bite is a salty spread of cheese on the soft, fluffy crumb. Erin has never tasted something so wonderful in her life.

"How is it?"

A moan escapes Erin's mouth. "Amazing."

Karl smirks and proceeds to consume his own portion of bread. Those slices, thick and fluffy, are enough to satisfy her belly for now. They sit silently by the crackling fire, the looming shadows cast upon the blanket of dry leaves, their only company.

"We should get to sleep," Karl says, dusting his hands and depositing the crumbs onto the ground. He removes his cloak and crumples it into a ball, tossing it to Erin.

Caught by surprise, she is met with a face full of fabric; it smells distinctly like ash, or soil after a refreshing drizzle.

Erin stares at it for a full second, before asking, "What's the purpose of—?"

"Pillow," Karl says. "Or blanket. Whatever you want. It's yours to use." Karl grabs his rucksack from beside the fire and digs around in its contents. "I'll keep the first watch."

Erin shakes her head. "No, *I'll* do it."

Karl pauses, glancing over at her and sizing her up. "Suit yourself. Just don't doze off, okay?"

He agreed rather readily, but both he and Erin know what this is: a test. It would be preposterous to trust the other so easily, having just met, especially when one may throw the other to the wolves—literally—the second they have to.

Karl will not sleep and Erin knows that, and Karl probably knows that *she* knows that he won't sleep. He will watch her when he thinks she has glanced away. Which is why his back is not to her but rather to the woods. Right now, to Karl, Erin is more dangerous than any other beast out there.

Erin remains seated by the fire, clutching Karl's coat to her body, tightening her grip when the drafts curl around her like nature's cold embrace. She gazes into the woods, kept awake only by the bite of the wind, ears pricked as she listens for tell-tale noises of wolves—or other dangerous beings—that may stalk the forest.

They are visited by fireflies descending upon their campfire, their gentle glows a sharp contrast to the fire's scorching brilliance. Harmless beings, bringing with them an illumination so beautiful they belong in a photograph to be displayed for all of eternity.

The moon hangs high above their heads, a glowing sphere weaving through tendrils of clouds. It's almost magical watching the stars twinkle not through thick iron bars, but through a frame of rustling leaves. What is it like on the moon? Is it as beautiful there? Maybe she should find a way up there someday.

When Erin deems the time to be appropriate, when the moon chooses to hide behind a veil of clouds, she shakes Karl awake. He pretends to rouse from his slumber, but the alertness in his piercing gaze and the sharpness of his voice belies his caution. As sleepy as Erin may be, she forces herself to stay awake, lest Karl approaches her with impure intentions.

She does not take her eyes off him, not for a full ten minutes at the very least. Karl sits by the log, bow in hand. He stares at the fire in rumination, as though he were slaving over the world's hardest question in unadulterated silence. Erin itches to ask what, but she is determined to put up as convincing a façade as her companion did.

Until she drifts off to dreamland, of course, tuckered out by the day's adventure. Lost to the world of clanking metal boots, the stench of rotten food, and the fear-filled eyes of that *rodent* as she left him to his fate.

# Chapter 3

## Town on the Edge

"Morning, sleepyhead."

Erin jolts awake and sits upright. Karl's coat tumbles off of her and pools around her thighs. When did she…? *How* did she…? Erin whips her head around, glancing at the crackling fire in the pit and the black pot just over it, to the man seated on a log with a ladle in hand.

Karl had already packed his rucksack, the bag now on the ground next to him. He stirs the small pot of soup over a cooking fire. When did he set that up?

"How?" Erin starts, rubbing at her eyes. "How did I fall asleep?"

"Exhaustion. Lack of willpower. Too trusting," Karl says knowingly. "Many reasons."

Erin runs her fingers along the hem of her tunic.

"Relax. I didn't do anything." Karl dips the ladle into the broth and fills a bowl. Rosemary sits on its surface, surrounded by white strips of meat and a handful of corn. The aroma is enough to make her salivate.

Karl hands her the bowl, and Erin stares into the cloudy suspension. She can only imagine how wonderful it would taste. Surely, it has to be better than the bitter stew served every other night back in the castle.

Karl sips at his own portion of soup, eyes peeking over the bowl. Watching her. The test is still on, it seems.

If so, Erin is not going to back down from this challenge. She tips the bowl and drinks up the broth. It scalds her tongue and throat, as though it were lighting a fire within her. She coughs violently, spewing corn to the ground. Karl bursts into laughter, soup splashing dangerously near the rim of his bowl.

"Slow down." Karl grins, wiping at his mouth with the back of his hand. "You're going to choke if you keep drinking like that."

Erin glares at him, still coughing and willing the pain to leave her be.

Karl gestures at the cauldron. "You can take more if you want. We have a lot."

His easy smile, the careless invitation, the innocuous front yet to be dropped. They are both still caught in each other's rhythm, in each other's waltz. Very well, Erin will take him up on that offer.

She refills her bowl, the steam curling around the ladle like tendrils of warmth. Erin blows on the surface and sips warily this time. The soup trickles down her throat, soothing and delicious. Karl is a wonderful cook, she decides.

After breakfast, before any curious critters arrive, Karl packs up and they are ready to leave.

"Where are we going now?"

"Hmm?" Karl turns back to her, a canteen of water dangling against his leg. "Cassia Springs."

"Cassia?" Erin has little knowledge of the world outside the castle. Its suffocating walls, the constant clanking of armour on stone tiles, the silence of the night, and the scampering of rat-people in the walls: that was all she knew.

"Just past the forest," Karl says. "It's a lovely town for people from all walks of life. Any race, any background, you're welcome there."

The tranquil forest is quiet in the morning, melodious birdsong an appropriate soundtrack as they journey down the path. Gravel crunches underfoot, the leaves rustle in the trees, and squirrels squeak in the canopies. Karl regales her with stories of adventure in the woods, of life in the town. Erin nods and listens with rapt attention, fascinated by all the experiences that she had never had.

"I managed to escape in the end," Karl says, finishing off yet another tale that kept Erin entertained on the long walk to Cassia Springs. "Almost broke my shin, though."

Erin glances down at his leg. "Really?"

"It was a long time ago. I didn't actually break it in the end."

Erin has no idea what it is like to break a bone. It would probably hurt so incredibly much and be very inconvenient. An inability to walk, let alone run, would put an early end to her quest to journey across the lands.

"Anyway, what's your story?" Karl asks. "I've told you about my grand escapades, tales of a dashing hero…"

"I'm just an ordinary girl."

"Surely you don't expect me to believe that."

"Why is it so hard to believe?"

"An ordinary girl like you wouldn't be running through the woods with nothing on you," Karl says. "Especially not the Forest of Fairies. You've seen the beasts. If you live around here, you'd know about them. No *normal* person would dare enter these woods without some form of defence."

Karl has a right head on his shoulders after all.

"It's true that I'm not from these parts," Erin says finally after a lull. "We were attacked last night, and my companion was murdered."

Karl glances away. A moment of silence reigns over them. "I'm sorry for your loss."

Erin regards him with curiosity. What's he got to be sorry for?

"You want to talk about it?" Karl asks. "It must not have been easy for you."

"Not really. Everything happened in a flash, and that was that. Elias was stabbed, and I had to run for my life."

"Elias? A friend of yours?"

"Younger brother. Elias was my younger brother."

Karl nods. "I see."

They fall back into a relative silence, occasionally broken by small talk. The tension between them grew considerably, thick enough now to slice with a knife. Erin does not mind; she does not have to speak to Karl, and she won't have to disclose any more details, any more lies that may easily slip out her.

Very soon, they come to a bluff. A large lake lies beyond the cliff's edge, its shores covered in grass scattered with all colours imaginable. From their vantage point, a mountain range is clearly visible, its peaks hidden by drifting sheets of clouds. At its base is a sprawling town, small houses clustered on the rolling hills.

"That's Cassia. That over there," he says, a finger outstretched. "We'll have to cross Lake Cordelia, then we'll reach it in no time."

"How do you propose we do that?" Erin's gaze sweeps across the empty shore. Apart from a few torn jetties, it lacks any defining features.

"Easy. We ride Nessi."

"Nessi?"

Karl grabs a thick vine from the cliff wall and tests its strength. Gingerly, he lowers himself over the edge, gripping the tendril tightly. He navigates the rocky wall, feet tapping gently across the rough surface, bounding from grassy outcrop to grassy outcrop.

"You all right there?" Karl calls from a platform, his hands on his hips. "Need a hand, princess?"

"Don't call me that."

Karl whistles at her, sounding almost like a taunt.

Erin bites her lip. She escaped from the dungeons, ran from a bunch of armoured guards, *and* avoided death by wolf. This can hardly be a challenge in the face of her accomplishments.

Erin glances back at a forest bustling with life. The King would not let her go so easily, not when he commands a legion of knights that can track her down. She has to go now, before her apprehension kicks in.

She touches the vine, hairy against her fingertips. Taking a deep breath, Erin carefully shifts into a more comfortable position, trying to imitate Karl.

The climb strains her arms, and her muscles are already complaining by the first platform. Karl yells encouragement from the outcrop below, but Erin ignores him. She does not need the pity of a stranger. She continues at her same pace, gritting her teeth and clenching her fingers around the vines. Her feet kick against the face of the cliff in desperate search for footholds.

All of a sudden, she misses. Erin shrieks, her sole gliding against the rocks. The sudden, extreme motion almost rips her pants by the seams. She scrabbles for traction, the blood coursing through her ears drowning out all else.

Erin has got this entirely under control. Her arms tremble, about to give out—but she has got it... under... control...

"Ellie! Jump and I'll catch you!"

Catch her? Is he insane? The impact of her fall would send them tumbling over the edge to their bloody demise.

Erin's foot slips even farther, forcing a gasp. Her fingers are losing their grip on the smooth vine, and her thighs are shaking.

"Jump! Don't worry about me!"

*To survive, one must learn to take risks.*

Erin takes a deep breath and lets herself go. Her stomach drops as she plummets, the rush of air light on her skin like ribbons of satin. Her fall is broken by two arms and a warm body.

"Uh-oh..."

Those are Karl's last words before Erin is once more taken by the wind. Their screams echo through the thicket, clouds of leaves smacking them in their faces. Branches scratching their arms and legs.

They land in a bush, with leaves so slim, so razor-edged, they cut you if you so much as touch them. Erin and Karl are caught in a heap of tangled limbs, so intricately intertwined that it proves a challenge to extricate one from the other.

Somehow, they escape the bush, tending to their raw skin and fresh cuts. Erin rubs at a bloody nick on her calf, while Karl nurses a tender arm.

"I told you we would fall," Erin mutters, rather glad that she walked away with no more than what she had.

Karl shrugs. "I'd prefer to think of it as a shortcut."

His bag and quiver of arrows remain magically unharmed, but his bow was snapped and splintered. Karl inspects his losses, pursing his lips as he readjusts the strapped weapon.

"I could always get a new one from Mel," Karl says. "That's going to put a dent in my wallet, though."

Erin nods. Mel...? Wallet...? What are those?

"Now." Karl turns to the lake. "Let's get over there, shall we?"

THE LAKE IS BIGGER than Erin thought. It looked vast when she had seen it from the vantage of the bluff, but as they got closer, it became bigger and bigger, the water now stretching as far as the eye can see. Flocks of birds hover near the surface, snatching up easy prey with a snap of their beaks. Dragonflies just as large as they flit from place to place, their paper-thin wings flapping at sonic speeds.

"Cool, eh?" Karl smirks at the apparent wonder on Erin's face.

"It is. I've never seen anything like it."

Karl laughs. "Where'd you come from? The desert?"

Erin has never seen the desert in her life—she's only ever read about it in books. Boundless dunes and golden sand, populated with strange plants called cacti, sprouting flowers and needle-like leaves. She frowns.

"Probably not the desert then." Karl scratches at his stubble. "Maybe the fjord?"

"No, I just came from another town. You know the King's castle?"

"Wait, you *lived* there?" Karl gape his mouth at her. Erin holds up her hands, shaking her head furiously.

"No, not there. I came from another town *beyond* there. Just outside of the kingdom."

"Oh." Karl presses his lips into a thin line. "I see."

"The King is a despicable man," Erin bites out. "He cares for no-one but himself. If anyone gets in his way, he will cut them down with no hesitation."

"That's some intense hatred, huh?"

Erin huffing. "I hate dwelling on the past. We should focus on getting across the lake."

Karl bows in jest. "As you wish, princess."

"Don't call me that."

They approach the jetty after a while, all the while enduring the relentless blaze of the sun's glaring rays. The place has almost been entirely reclaimed by nature; moss and weeds curl around rotten planks of wood. Bugs make their home in the damp wood, as do the spiders, their silken webs stretching from plank to plank, with no predator in sight. Best carry on before they return from the hunt or whatever it is that spiders get up to.

Erin and Karl stride up to the farthest end of the jetty. A breeze picks up, tousling Erin's hair and rippling the water. The reeds sway and rustle.

"What do we do now?" she asks.

"We have to call Nessi. But she only responds to a certain song."

"Does she?"

"Of course. Everyone in Cassia knows it."

Erin steps back as Karl begins to sing. His voice travels far out across the lake, smooth and soft, just like when he talks. The song is in a language she does not understand, but that doesn't matter. What matters is whether Nessi arrives or not.

As Karl hits a high note, a shadow emerges from the depths, its long neck cutting through the water's surface. Shiny scales cover its body, glimmering pinkly in the light of the sun. Nessi swims over, flippers almost still as it glides across the lake. Karl ends his song.

"Karl Derrickson of Cassia Springs," Nessi says. "How may I assist you today?"

Nessi's lilting voice was like the whisper of a refreshing spring zephyr. Karl approaches the creature, holding out a hand, which Nessi merely gazes at serenely.

"I would like to return to Cassia," he says, "with this fair maiden who now journeys with me."

*Fair maiden.* Is that not what knights call their princesses in all the stories that Erin has read? She resists her urge to scrunch her nose up at such a comment. Nessi glances at Erin, then back to Karl.

"She is not a resident of Cassia Springs. I'm afraid I cannot grant her free passage."

"I'll pay for her. Don't worry about it."

As much as Erin dislikes the idea of owing debts, she doubts she has much choice in the matter. She must get away from the castle as quickly as possible, before the guards come calling. Perhaps she can repay Karl at a later date.

Nessi lowers its head, and Karl retrieves something from his bag. A gleaming ring of sorts with a golden band. Nessi gently bites the ring, before tucking it beneath its scales. It turns, backing up close enough to the jetty so that they may get on.

Karl makes a sweeping gesture. "After you."

Erin smiles. "Thanks."

Chivalry can get you far. Erin clambers onto Nessi's body, gripping the scales and hauling herself onto Nessi's bulk. Karl hops on after, and Nessi departs, making for the town of Cassia just beyond the lake's expanse.

"THANKS, NESSI," KARL calls, waving to Nessi from Cassia's pier. "I'll be seeing you."

Nessi growls in response, and it sinks back into the water, till no trace of the creature remains. The pier they disembark on is thriving. Sailors rush about, carrying cargo and crates. Small boats bob on the water, tied to the jetty with thick ropes. Erin takes care not to trip over haphazardly-placed barrels as she follows Karl to the centre of the pier.

"Hey, Karl!"

A girl walks up to them, a bandana wrapped around her head to keep her curly, blonde hair in place. She hugs a bag of an ugly floral pattern to her chest.

Karl straightens his shoulders "Oh, uh... Hi, Susie. What's that you got there?"

"Huh? This?" Susie jerks her chin at the bag. "A dirk."

"A dirk? For Mitch?"

"Yeah. And you know how Mitch gets when I'm late." Susie sighs. "Well, I've gotta get going. I'll be seeing you around! Bye, Karl! See ya, chick!"

"What—!"

With that, Susie departs, waving enthusiastically as she sets off for the port. Karl sighs. Erin tilts her head.

"Chick? I'm human, though."

Karl pinches the bridge of his nose. "Don't—She's just messing around. And thirsty."

"Thirsty? Doesn't this place have water?"

Karl massages his temples. "Let's just go."

The town is bigger than anywhere that Erin has ever been—though she hasn't been to many places. The size of the houses and establishments are just right for people their height. Much better than the immense castle that the King ruled from. Banners hang over their heads, decorating archways and storefronts; posters had been slapped on walls and trumpeting youths declared a festival that is soon to come.

"A festival?" Erin wonders.

"Cassia Springs' anniversary." Karl clicks his tongue. "Celebration of our liberation from the Overlord."

"Overlord?"

"Legend has it that a dragon lived on Mount Blaze." Karl points at a volcano standing, imposingly, a distance away. "It reigned over Cassia Springs with an iron fist. Then a valiant knight journeyed to the top of the volcano and slew it."

"He was hailed a hero?"

"Yeah. I think it's a load of bullshit, though. I don't believe it one bit." Karl shrugs. "But the festival's tomorrow, and there will be a parade and everything."

Perhaps Erin should check it out if she has the time, as limited as it is. The King has undoubtedly ordered a search for her. Cassia Springs is much too near to the castle to give Erin peace of mind. She should ask for a map, some money...

Karl turns down a side street, a narrow path crowded by bags of trash and puddles of waste. Compared to those on the main street, these shops are smaller, dimmer, more derelict, as though their cheer had been sapped dry. A seagull takes to the skies upon their approach.

"Where are we headed?" Erin asks.

"My house."

"You live among these..."

"Next to a poppy den."

A poppy den? Poppies are flowers, are they not? Don't they belong in the wild plains?

Karl knocks thrice on a door. A muffled voice calls from behind.

"Password?"

Karl glances over at Erin and hums. "You know what? It's Ellie."

Erin widens her eyes as the rusted door opens, metal scraping against the wooden floorboards. A short man sporting a beard, dressed in gnomish wear, greets them from the other side of the doorway. Erin does not fail to notice the gleaming blade in his hand.

"Karl!" the dwarf cries, tottering back into the dingy room, voice scratchy. "Welcome back!"

"Glad to see you too, Mel." Karl looks like he would have scooped his friend into a hug if not for the knife in Mel's hands. He turns to Erin and makes a sweep at the door. "Right, into the Hatchet with you."

"The Hatchet?"

"Name o' the shop," Mel replies helpfully. "I sell all sorts o' shit 'ere. Bound to be somethin' you'd like."

The shop is nothing but a hole in the wall, hardly ideal for conducting business. The narrow entranceway opens up to a tiny room illuminated by the flame of a lantern. Blades glint upon the racks crowded into a tiny recess, while crossbows and javelins are displayed behind the counter. A set of stairs, cordoned off by a thin chain, spirals up to a higher floor.

"Ellie the lass?"

Karl grins mischievously. "Yes."

"About that." Erin holds up a hand. "Why is your password my name?"

"It's not yer name, lass," Mel says, his grin mirroring Karl's. "It's what comes before."

Erin raises a brow. That is rather smart of them.

"What brings ya here, eh? You Karl's girlfriend?"

"Girlfriend?" Erin frowns.

"Nope." Karl shakes his head. "I'm not interested in dating now, Mel."

Mel chuckles, flashing a golden tooth. "Just teasin'. Was funny how ya swore off datin' aft' the way Susie dumped ya ass."

"Wasn't she the girl we just met?" Erin asks.

Karl scratches his head. "Yes."

"Let me tell ya, lassie. A tale of woe and utter embarrassment—"

"Please. Spare her the details." Karl places his backpack on the ground and unstraps his bow, splintered down the middle. Mel eyes it with absolute disgust.

"You fuckin' broke the Artemis?"

"It's not my fault! I was saving Ellie!"

Mel's frustration cools to a simmer. He sighs. "Give it here."

Karl does as he is told. Mel clucks his tongue. He speaks but not in a language that Erin understands. Elven mixed with a tad of Common, perhaps? Erin surveys the room instead, inspecting all the various weaponry Mel has on display. Longswords, broadswords, rapiers, knives, daggers, and even staves, all crowded around a heavyset door behind the counter.

Could she, perhaps, nick one of these? Will Mel notice? There's no knowing what threats she will face from here on out, and it is highly likely that the Captain and the rest of the Guard will be hunting her. A weapon—any weapon—would be extremely handy if it came to that...

"Thanks a lot, Mel."

"It's all right." Mel rocks on his chair, legs barely long enough to throw his feet up on the counter. "Why don'tcha show the lass to yer quarters, eh? Give 'er someplace to sleep t'night."

"Right," Karl says. He jerks his chin to the staircase. "Let's get going, princess."

Princess. That nickname again. Erin sighs; Karl has ignored her requests to stop using it, so there is nothing she can do to dissuade him. "To your quarters? Is it not...unseemly for a woman to enter a man's room?"

"You can always sleep out here if you'd like." Karl gestures at the shop. "Besides, we've got a mattress, so there's no need to worry about chastity and all that shite."

Erin wrinkles her nose at the idea, but it's not like she has a choice. She follows him up the stairs, boards creaking with every step. They come to a long corridor flanked by doors, as dusty and musty as the rest of the building. He leads her to a small room, one that smells distinctly of Karl.

The room is sparsely-furnished—lacking chairs and tables. A wardrobe stands in the corner, cobwebs spun between its sides and the walls. The narrow cot by the window holds a tattered mattress, no better than the thin rug beneath it.

"Do you never clean this place?"

"I do whenever I come back from my trips." Karl shrugs. He walks over to the wardrobe and pulls it open. Erin half-expected a skeleton to tumble out, bones clattering to the ground; however, there is nothing besides a few ratty outfits and another rolled-up mattress.

"You can take the bed, and I'll sleep here." Karl lugs the mattress out of the wardrobe and lays it out on the rug.

"Thank you."

Sunlight wanes as the blazing orb sets behind the tall buildings that surround their little hideout. It now casts a squarish glow upon the floor.

"Let's go out for a little night stroll," Karl says. "We need to get you new clothes, too."

A splendid idea. Changing up her appearance could keep her under the radar for just that much longer before the guards find out where she's been hiding.

"All right, let's go," Erin says, striding towards the door. Karl stops her with a teasing whistle.

"Do you even have any money to pay for it all?"

Money? Erin spins on her heels, giving him a quizzical look. Karl folds his arms, a smug grin on his face.

He pinches thin air, rubbing his fingers together. "Money. To pay. Cha-ching."

Cha-ching? What does that mean?

"I don't have this... money of which you speak."

Karl raises a brow. "Wow, I don't know where you came from, but here in Cassia, we need to give something in return if you want to take someone else's things. We call it 'making a purchase'."

Making a purchase?

"Well, if you don't have money... I guess I'll pay." Karl pauses, then corrects himself. "Actually, Mel'll pay. He earns big bucks from his business."

"Bucks? Are we stealing his deer from him?"

Karl laughs. "Nah. I'm talking about money, man."

"You could have been clearer."

Karl grins. "Now I'm just imagining Mel fighting deer. Anyway, I'm sure this plan will work. He always gives money if Susie's the one asking for it."

"You are such a despicable man. Is that all women are to you?"

"Susie didn't mind. All you have to do is to just ask, and you get money. For no cost at all."

Erin sighs. As long as that's all there is to it.

# Chapter 4

## The Night of the Parade

"How do I look?" Erin pats her new brown tunic. It ends right below her waist, over a pair of beige, tight-fitting pants.

Karl whistles. "Gorgeous."

They pay for the clothes and leave the store. Erin makes a mental note to dispose of her old attire a fair distance from her new temporary living quarters. The King's Guard are certainly capable creatures, especially the Captain.

The sun has long since set, but the town does not sleep. The high street is as crowded as ever, from last-minute rehearsals and decorating to shoppers darting from shop to shop, enticed by promotions and discounts. Children dash about, playing tag and laughing with each other.

It sends a pang through Erin's heart.

"Hey, come on over."

Karl jogs ahead to the pier. Most of the boats are docked, ropes keeping them tied in place. The row of taverns by the lakeside bursts with raucous merriment. The lake ripples, water splashing against the legs of the jetties. Across the water, a cliff above, the blue of fireflies surrounds the great canopies of the forest they left behind.

Even farther back, hidden by the trees, is Erin's former prison. One she would have been born and died in had she simply accepted her fate and not tried to escape.

"What are we doing here?" Erin asks.

"To soak in the sea breeze." Karl stands at the edge of a jetty with his hands on his hips. "Lake breeze. Whatever."

"But..."

"But what?" Against the glow of blinking fairy lights, and the flickering shimmer of moonbeams on the water's surface, Karl looks almost ethereal. He pins her with an intense gaze, his hand an invitation to see a whole new world.

Who is Erin to refuse?

Karl may live in a seedy lodging, may fraternise with shady associates, but he does not threaten her with confinement. He is not at all like the King.

Erin takes Karl's hand. She had hoped to see the world one day, on her own terms.

But this is nice too.

BREAKFAST WAS A SIMPLE affair. Karl took her to a café just around the corner on the main street. A dainty place: small tables draped with chequered tablecloths, wicker chairs mighty comfortable to sit upon. Erin wolfs down her fluffy muffins and pancakes drenched in syrup, the sweetest food that she's ever tasted.

"How'd you like it?" Karl asks, stuffing a muffin into his mouth.

"It's good." Better than what they served in the dungeons.

"Glad to hear that."

The lake glistens in the light of the warm morning sun. Gulls soar overhead, wings stretched and riding the waves of the wind. Fishing boats are already out and about, dotting the expanse of the lake. As they walk along the pier, Erin spots Nessi hard at work, taking the people of Cassia from jetty to jetty across the water.

"Nice, isn't it?" Karl raises an arm to shield his eyes from the light. "Waking up to this every morning, feeling the sun on my face... it's really a blessing."

"It is."

Silence overcomes them briefly, a silence that Erin soaks in. A pleasant silence broken by the lap of the water, the call of birds, the whistle of the wind.

"Anyway, what're you planning?" Karl asks. "Are you staying here? Or leaving? You were on a journey, weren't you?"

"I am, and I've got to get going." *Before the King's legions come hunting.*

"What? So soon?"

Erin shrugs. "As soon as possible."

"I don't know why you're in such a hurry, but..." Karl scratches his head. "How about after the festival? One more day couldn't hurt. You can always leave tomorrow morning."

She considered his proposition. There had been no movement from the forest, no disturbances on the lake. The forest may have been a long road to travel by foot for people as tiny as they are, but the guards could have crossed it by now. Maybe they have not made their move. If so, what are they waiting for?

What is the King's plan here?

"Ellie?"

Erin shakes her head. "I suppose... one more day couldn't... hurt."

A grin grows on Karl's face, so bright it's almost blinding.

"Well, the festival takes off around evening," Karl says. "We can explore the town today or... take a boat out to the lake."

"Let's explore the town." Erin genuinely wants to see what more Cassia Springs has to offer. However, that is not her only intention. Karl is most certainly a citizen of this town—he is probably a custodian of its secrets. Hidden pathways, transportation, the general geography...

If Erin ever needs to run, she needs to know this place well enough to make her escape. At least, more than her enemy does. As long as she can outsmart them, outrun them, then...

Karl takes her by the wrist and drags her over to the town square like an excited schoolboy. Or rather, what Erin thinks an excited schoolboy would look like. Perhaps she would compare him to Elias instead. How his tail would snap about or how his whiskers would twitch whenever Erin read out to him her fantasy books.

How strange. Erin had read about the effects of trauma and the lingering distress of watching someone die before your very eyes. Elias' probable death, getting snatched up by the troll chef, his terrified screams...

They never stayed.

Just images and sounds waiting to be forgotten.

Erin chases those thoughts from her mind. She is no longer a prisoner to that castle anymore. She is the captain of her own ship, and right now, Karl is the gust of wind, taking her wherever at his whim and fancy.

"THIS IS THE TRAIN STATION."

Cassia Springs' station has seen better days. The platform is chipped and dirty, the walls are graffitied, and the posters are stripped from wooden boards till they are nothing but dangling scraps of paper.

The primary workers are zombies. Or, more specifically, the zombies of fairies, elves, and all the other races that live in this fair town. Janitors, conductors, what-have-yous. They greet you with slurred words and unblinking, unfocused eyes; their lines are so obviously rehearsed that they hardly feel sincere.

The tracks run along a gravel path, away from the town, past lush, green plains, before disappearing into a tunnel carved into a hill. Erin has never seen a train before—this could prove to be an enlightening experience.

"Where does the train go, and when does it come?" she asks.

"At midnight. On the dot. As for where it would take you... it takes you wherever you want to go. It ends at Astra, though, so if you want to go elsewhere, you're gonna have to switch trains—or take a plane."

"A plane?"

Karl purses his lips. "It's, like, this big metal thing in the sky with wings."

"Like fairy wings?"

"No, like... big metal *wings*."

Erin giggles. "Not good at explaining, are you?"

Karl sighs. "Maybe I wouldn't have to explain if you knew something as basic as a plane."

A moment of silence hangs over them. He scratches his head, gaze dropped.

"Hey, I'm sorry. I..."

"No, it's fine." Erin shakes her head. She approaches the edge of the platform, trying to peek into the darkness of the tunnel. Karl moves to stand behind her, exhaling deeply.

"Sorry for saying that. I wasn't thinking."

Erin humphs.

"I'll make it up to you."

Erin scrunches her nose. She hardly needs his pity, his... scorn, or whatever. Karl made an honest mistake; he apologized and expressed remorse. She assured him that it was fine.

She is not going to butter him up.

"No need."

Erin turns on her heels, but Karl stops her with a timid question.

"Are you... mad at me?"

"Does it look like I'm mad?" Erin suppresses her growing scowl, the bubbling frustration from the pit of her gut. Why is he harping on about this?

"To be entirely honest? Yes."

"I just think it's annoying that you'd apologize so much."

Still, Karl looks like a kicked puppy with those drooped shoulders and sullen gaze. Could she turn this into a win-win situation?

"How about this?" she says. Karl looks up, tilting his head in question. "You accompany me on the train and take me to Astra tonight, and I'll forgive whatever you just did."

"Take you to Astra?" Karl crosses his arms. "I mean, it's just a straight journey from one end of the line to another."

"But I know nothing about this land." Erin gestures to the station. "Wouldn't it be a stain on your conscience to let a helpless girl go out to such a faraway place all by herself?"

Karl considers it, shifting his weight from one foot to the next.

"All I need to do is to get settled in Astra. After that, you can go straight home."

"All right." Karl holds up his hands. "Just... Just to Astra, right?"

Erin beams, her spirits lifted. She, quite literally, just secured her ticket out of here and far away where the King cannot pursue her.

As soon as Karl finishes purchasing the tickets for tonight's Express, the duo walk away from the dingy station and back to the high street of the city. It is mostly cordoned off with ribbons tied to the slim bodies of streetlamps. Many people gather under the light of the setting sun, men and women of all ages and races, chatting happily as they await the start of the procession.

"Shall we get dinner first?" Karl asks. His words are looser; his tone, less serious.

At the mention of dinner, Erin's stomach growls. A fluffy pancake or some broth sounds good about now.

Erin nods. "Where to?"

Karl's easy grin returns to his face. "There are pubs by the pier. They should still be open at this time."

THE PUB THAT KARL INTRODUCES her to is aptly named the Fat Fairy, owned by one of the burliest fairies Erin ever met. He goes by the name of Avery, a silver beard tumbling freely over his chest. He serves them in the gruffest voice but with the kindest tone.

"Enjoy your meal, lad and lass."

Erin responds with the same polite smile, and Karl forks out the money which Avery collects. He shambles back to the counter and takes another order. Erin looks down at her fish fillet, breaded skin golden under the dim light. Karl reaches over and snatches one of her chips.

Erin merely watches as Karl withdraws his hand, stuffing the stick of potato into his mouth.

"Why'd you steal that? You have your own."

Karl licks his finger. "It's fun."

"What's so fun about eating other people's food?"

"It's the stealing that's fun. Go on. Try it."

Erin furrows her brows. There is clearly no logic behind whatever he had just said, but since he invited her to even out his debt... she has no reason to refuse. Erin plucks a chip from his plate and stares at it for a good while before meeting Karl's expectant gaze.

That gaze soon turns into a frown. "That's more anticlimactic than I thought it would be."

"I'm not sure what you expected. I'm just taking your food and you're letting me."

Karl chuckles.

They dig into their meal, as delicious as any other would be outside that hellhole castle. Erin can hardly get enough of the crunchy crust, the tenderness of the fish within its crispy exterior. The chips may be nothing more than deep-fried salty potatoes, but they are still better than stale bread and lean meat.

By the time they step out and onto the main street, the procession has already begun. Erin gasps, watching a bevy of horses, draped in colourful cloths, strut down the path. Their riders are all dolled up, their gaudy sequined outfits shimmering in the light of the moon and the festive bulbs scattered along the roads.

"This is beautiful."

Dancers show off their sparkly costumes, snapping their fingers and flicking puffs of azure will-o-wisps to illuminate their audience. Erin oohs at the glow, reaching out to touch it. The light prances around her finger, before fizzling out and vanishing.

"Look." Karl raises an arm above their heads, pointing at the clusters of twinkling stars.

A display of fireworks: flowers of red, yellow, and green bloom in the black of the night sky, showering them with pixie dust. Explosions ring out amidst the grand music of the marching band. The procession carries on with a near-endless line of horses, dancers, and floats. Erin wishes that this moment would last forever.

Unfortunately, Fate has something else in store.

A shriek resounds from the lake. The festivities halt immediately. The music stops, and so do the dancers. Every participant's gaze is cast at the lake—at Nessi, who slumps into the water and lies, unmoving, on its surface.

Behind Nessi's corpse, now shoved carelessly aside by its killer, is a horde of armoured knights marching towards them, their bodies clad with steel glimmering under the moonlight. Every single one of them is armed with a musket, their barrels glinting menacingly. They stop a distance from the pier, the water level at their waists. The Captain raises his arm.

Erin cannot move. She stands, rooted to the spot, watching that arm. Silence blankets the town, and no-one dares to speak.

When the Captain brings his arm down, following a sharp battle cry, the first musket fires.

A piercing crack rings out on the pier. Fairies take off into the sky, wings fluttering and scattering dust with each frantic beat. Elves and dwarves duck into alleyways, their hats pulled over dipped heads.

"Ellie, we have to go!" Karl grabs Erin's wrist and drags her into the dispersing crowd, diving down a side street and towards their hideout. People cower in the alcoves, whimpering with their hands over their heads. Karl raps his knuckles on the door.

"Password!"

Karl snarls. "You know what? It's we're going to fucking die!"

The door swings open and Karl yanks her in, kicking the door shut on the foot of a drifter. The drifter screams and tries to force the door open, squeezing half his body through despite Karl's insistent hold.

A bullet sings by Erin's ear. Blood blossoms on the drifter's forehead, trickling down his nose. In the next moment, he slumps against the door and Karl shoves his twitching body out. Karl slams the door shut, shunting the lock in place.

"God!" Karl snaps.

Erin glances back at Mel, who stands on his chair, a smoking revolver in hand. He tosses to Karl the hunter's mended bow, Artemis, as well as a quiver of arrows.

"Ya want a knife, lass?" Mel asks.

It was not a question, as Erin soon learns. Mel chucks her a knife sheathed in leather, which she fumbles with.

"Okay, Karl, what the bloody fuck is 'appenin' outside?"

Karl heads up the stairs, dashing off to his room, and Erin follows him.

"Uh... the King's attacking. And I have no idea why." Karl throws the door open, only to see the single scarlet eye staring back at him from under a knight's helmet.

"Karl!" Erin slams into Karl from behind, sending the both of them sprawling to the ground. The shoddy windows explode, glass raining everywhere, jagged shards cutting into Erin's neck and arms.

Karl shoves Erin off him and grabs his pack. He pulls her to her feet.

"Come on!" he shouts. "Let's go!"

"Go? Go where?"

They barrel through the doorway, barely avoiding a grubby hand forcing its way through the shattered window. Karl and Erin take the stairs two at a time, footsteps so heavy that Erin fears the staircase will break beneath their stomps. Mel waits at the bottom, unlocking and pulling open a door that leads even farther into the ground.

Erin grabs Karl's arm. "They're looking for me. We have to run. We have to get out of here."

"Looking for you? What does that mean?" Karl asks, his knitted brows betraying the confusion concealed by his anxiety.

Before Erin can answer, a crack of wood forces her to face the door. Fear spikes through her as she sees the splintering of the planks, and a terror-filled eye peeking through the hole. A bloodied arm sticks through another hole in the middle of the door.

"Less talking, more walking," Mel urges, gesturing at the tunnel. "In here!"

"Where does it lead?" Erin asks.

"Outta town."

Karl slams the back door just before the front door snaps off its hinges and bodies storm in. Killer knights or desperate drifters, Erin does not know. She follows Mel down the steps till they reach a narrow corridor smelling of musk and booze.

The corridor twists and turns, its walls lined with a nasty, green mould. The ceiling shakes every few seconds, showering them with clouds of dust. Mel's wings flutter faster as he darts on over to the end of the corridor, towards a ladder leading to a hatch.

Mel hovers there, his ear pressed up against the wood.

"Lots o' runnin' an' gunshots out there," Mel says. "Ya wanna get to the Midnight Express, ya gotta move fast, ya hear?"

"Wait, what about you, Mel?" Karl asks.

Mel chuckles, as though the prospect of leaving is unthinkable. "Me? I'm stayin'. I grew up here in Cassia. Ain't gon' run just 'cause o' some baddies."

"But..."

"But nothin'," Mel says adamantly. "I'm gonna cover ya till ya reach the station, then that's where we'll part ways."

Mel lays a palm on the hatch. "On the count of three. One... two..."

In one swift move, he pushes it open, revealing a clear, black sky, with nary a wispy cloud in sight. Mel clambers out of the hatch with Erin and Karl following right after.

The corridor brought them to the outskirts, filled with people fleeing from torn-apart houses, escaping towards the forest. Knights scoop fairies up into their hands, tearing their wings off before hurling them aside. The elves shoot from their trusty bows, but the arrows merely bounce off the knights' breastplates, clattering uselessly to the ground.

"There they are!" a raspy voice bellows.

Erin leaps over fallen bodies, over strips of shredded wings and bloodied limbs. Karl leads the way, making for the train station.

The only differences to how the station was that afternoon is that the zombies are now missing, and that the train is waiting on the platform. Its sleek, ghostly body is a stark contrast to the surroundings. Puffs of smoke billow from the engine's funnel, rising high into the air. The shrill shriek of its whistle alerts them of its imminent departure.

"We won't make it!" Erin pants.

A series of gunshots ring out from behind. Erin screams as bullets riddle the ground by her feet, smashing into the concrete and ricocheting off the cobblestone, shattering display windows and puncturing awnings.

"Take that, ya sleazy motherfuckers!" Mel roars.

More bangs resonate throughout the streets, followed by clangs and clinks. There is no time to glance back, not when their only chance at a getaway is taking off right in front of their eyes. They have only a short distance to cover, a couple of metres between themselves and the platform...

Karl's head snaps back at a sudden shout. From a gruff voice that Erin knows all too well. She grips his wrist, urging him forwards.

"Karl! What are you waiting for? The train's leaving!"

"Mel's hurt! We have to go back for him!"

"We can't! We have to leave, Karl! The train's going!" Erin tugs on his arm. The train is about to leave. It's moving away from the platform now, picking up speed...

"Let go of me—"

Erin glances back, meeting Mel's gaze for a single, silent moment before his tiny body is crushed under the boot of a knight. The crunch of bones under metal is enough for Karl to flinch, for Erin to drag him away from the approaching menace, towards the train station. If they go now, they might yet make it...

Erin sprints down the platform, her muscles pumping as hard as they can as they propel her forward. She yanks Karl with her as she leaps from the edge of the platform...

She tumbles onto the rumbling metal of the final carriage, Karl right there with her. The train moves off without a care in the world, chugging down the rails and leaving a town of death and destruction behind.

Erin takes a sharp breath. She draws her knees up to her chest and tries to calm her pounding heart. Karl kneels beside her, head lowered, his fists clenched against his thighs.

Neither speak for the longest time, not even as the train enters the tunnel. Not even as they head off to wherever next their great adventure would take them.

# Chapter 5

## A Breath of Fresh Air

"Here are your cabins. Thank you for travelling with the Midnight Express." A robot in a chambermaid's outfit greets them with a nasally voice, sounding almost human. She hands them each a keycard. Erin grasps her keycard with sweaty fingers and taps it on the reader. The reader blinks green, and the door clicks open.

Erin holds the card up against the light. How is it possible that something so small can be capable of so much?

"If you require assistance, you can summon me with a press of this button." The robot gestures to the bright red button by the door, a picture of a robot printed on its shiny surface. "There is one by the door in your room as well."

Erin nods, wondering just what this robot can help her with anyway. "Okay."

It welcomes them on board once more before rolling down the hallway. Erin glances at her companion, who has hardly spoken since they got on the train. Karl merely fidgets with his bow strapped to his pack.

"Let's get some sleep," Erin says. "Then we can decide what to do tomorrow."

Karl nods stiffly. He drags his feet into his cabin and shuts the door.

Erin stares at the closed door. *Mel died for their sakes, a wonderfully honourable death, as the books would say. Why is Karl sulking? He should be thankful that he had such a great friend.*

Erin taps her keycard against the reader again. The indicator flashes green, and she saunters in. The door swings shut and clicks behind her. She leans against the door and sighs, relief replacing her tension.

The cabin looks a lot cleaner and neater than where she had slept the night before. It is sparsely furnished, but it has everything she needs: a clean bed; a wardrobe; a desk and a chair; and a wide window curtained with flowing, floral cloth. Erin plods over to the bed and sinks into the soft mattress.

She lies there, unmoving, listening to the rumble of the train's wheels trundling against the tracks. How far from Cassia will the Midnight Express take them? She is no geography expert—the only worlds she lived in were spun from mere words and crude illustrations, mountains and valleys sprung from the recesses of her imagination.

How far is—

Erin frowns. What was that place called again? Karl mentioned it once, but it had slipped Erin's mind. She reaches for her ticket, the slip of paper almost shredded to ribbons.

"Astra," Erin reads aloud, staring at the name partially covered in dirt. Karl said that certain people aboard the train look at the tickets, to make sure you were not riding for free. Erin hopes they won't mind that she had scratched hers up.

Erin's arm drops, bouncing lightly on the bed, and she turns her head to the side. She takes a deep breath, filling her nostrils with the scent of cleanliness. The adrenaline drains from her body, leaving her in the throes of exhaustion. Erin closes her eyes and sighs, her chest rising and falling rhythmically.

Under the blanket of the night, clustered with magical, twinkling stars, Erin falls asleep to the lullaby loud in her ears—of terrified screams and the snap of bones against metal armour.

ERIN WAKES UP TO THE streams of the sun's rays filtering through the glass of the window. Her stomach rumbles, the fish that had served as her last meal no longer enough to sustain her. Where will she get food, though?

Maybe Karl knows. He is much more knowledgeable about this world than she is. Erin walks to the door and tries to push it open, only to find it immobile. Erin frowns. Is the door one-way like the one back in Karl's house? In that case, she needs to pull it.

However, tugging at the doorknob does not work either. The door remains firmly shut in Erin's face. Her pulse races, palms clammy with perspiration. How is she supposed to leave this place? Is she trapped?

Erin grits her teeth, gripping the knob tightly and giving it a sharp yank. The door does not budge. Is she supposed to kick it down? Is it malfunctioning?

Erin then spies the red button on the wall, the silhouette of the robot smiling up at her. Her last resort. As soulless as their mechanical hearts may be, the robots should be able to save her from this predicament. Quickly, she slams a fist on the button, and it glows a startling crimson.

Erin hears a muffled whirr, and a feminine voice speaks from behind the door.

"Good morning, dear guest," it asks. "How may I assist you today?"

"Um... how do you open the door?"

Erin's ears burn with embarrassment. She thanks her lucky stars that the robot's voice is emotionless—if she had to listen to a judging tone, she would never be able to get over it.

"Do you see the door handle on your end?" the robot asks patiently.

"Yes."

"Press it downwards."

As soon as Erin does so, she hears a click.

"Now, pull it towards you."

Erin pulls, just as she is told, the door swinging inwards and revealing a squarish robot in a frilly dress that ends just above its caterpillar wheels. Its nametag is pinned where its breast should be:

Belle. The robot bows and greets her with another good morning. A blocky smile appears on its screen for a face.

"Is there anything else I can assist you with?" Belle asks.

As curious as Erin is about the robots, she has more important matters to attend to. "No, nothing."

Belle flashes another digital smile and rolls away, down the hallway, and into the next carriage.

Erin turns back to Karl's door and raps her knuckles upon it. She hears a thump from within, then frantic footsteps. The door swings open, and Karl appears on the other end. His hair is dishevelled, his eyes bloodshot and sunken in his skull.

"Good morning," Erin says, wincing at the growl of her stomach. How embarrassing. "Are you hungry?"

Karl blinks, a blank look plastered on his face. Erin waits, somewhat curious about his demeanour. Why has he changed so much since the day before? Karl was cheery and full of pep, but now he seems to be nothing more than a husk, a shell.

They escaped, did they not? With every minute, they are getting farther and farther away from the devastated town of Cassia. They left the land ravaged by the knights, leaving the clutches of the King.

So why is Karl so... sorrowful?

"I'm not very hungry, but I guess I can get breakfast with you."

Erin beams. "Okay. Where do we have to go? Do they serve food on the train?"

Karl leads the way, travelling down carriage after carriage of cabins, through cabins from economic to deluxe. What the difference is, though, Erin has no idea. Eventually, they arrive at a carriage full of dining tables, surfaces polished till Erin can see every minute detail of her face reflected on them, and chairs fitted with fluffy cushions.

Most importantly, however, they have windows. Large windows that stretch from the ceiling to the floor, through which guests can be entertained by Mother Nature's wonders. Phoenixes fly beside the train, tails of fire trailing behind them. A herd of cockatrice dash alongside the carriage, darting beneath leaves and behind trees.

"May I see your ticket, please?"

The robot attending to them is wearing a tuxedo. Its name—Brendan—is printed on its nametag. Erin and Karl hand it their tickets. To Erin's delight, Brendan does not once flinch at the torn remains of hers. Once their validity is confirmed, Brendan leads them to a table, and Erin slides happily into her seat.

"Please, do take your time. I will attend to you shortly."

With that, Brendan takes off, swivelling on its single wheel as it rushes to entertain other guests. Erin flips through the menu, mouth watering at the pictures of various dishes, from the plumpness of roast chickens, to the swirl of broth in pots, with boiled vegetables peeking out from the soup.

"Pick whatever you like." Karl slumps back into his chair. Erin does not notice, her mind occupied with nothing but food. Sausages, lobsters, brisket... there are far too many choices to settle on just one!

"I want this, this..." Erin shows Karl the menu, almost like an excited child. "And this. Oh, and the fruit punch."

Karl shakes his head ever so slightly. "I don't have the money for that. You're going to have to decide on one."

"Money?" Erin vaguely recalls having heard that word before.

"We need to pay, Ellie."

"What does that mean?"

"It means we..." Karl scratches his head. "We need to give something in exchange for the food."

"Why can't we just ask for it?"

Karl shrugs. "People want to get something out of giving you food, I suppose. They need to survive in this world too."

Erin frowns. She does not quite understand, but if Karl says so...

She decides on the grilled ham sandwich, and Karl places the order for her. Brendan jots it down on its notepad and zips towards the kitchen, its wheel noiseless on the soft carpet.

Erin turns to look out the window, enraptured by the flock of cockatrices keeping up with the zooming train. She snaps her head back at Karl's sudden cough.

"How was your sleep?" Karl asks.

"It was amazing," Erin gushes. "The bed was so soft, and the window was *big*! It was so clean and—"

"Sounds like you had fun."

Erin nods vigorously, grinning from ear to ear. "I fell asleep as soon as I laid on the bed, but it was lovely. There were so many things I've never seen before, like this bucket that I can collect water in and..."

"A bathtub?"

Erin frowns. "Maybe. I don't know."

Karl chuckles hollowly. "Yeah, it's probably a bathtub. Have you never seen a bathtub before?"

"No. I only bathed in this pool of water back home. It kept getting greener and greener, though."

Karl gapes. "The water was green?"

"Yes." *Is there anything strange about that?*

Erin's food arrives: sandwiches of an incredible size burst with strips of ham and melted cheese. She digs in immediately, chomping down on the bread, not even flinching as the heat scorches her tongue. No amount of heat could stop her from filling her empty stomach.

"Do you want one?" Erin asks, gesturing at the other sandwich left on her plate.

Karl shakes his head. "I'm fine."

"But you haven't eaten anything since last night." Erin slides the plate over to him. "Have at least one."

Conflict crosses Karl's face as he stares at the sandwich. Eventually, he reaches for it and puts it to his mouth, nibbling on the bread and the cheese and the ham. Satisfied, Erin sips her fruit punch, gagging at the taste.

"What's wrong?"

"It's sour."

"Fruit punch is supposed to be sweet."

Erin puckers her lips. "Sour."

"Well, you ordered it."

"Can't we ask them to change it?"

"Nope."

Karl seems to have regained some of his vitality since eating the sandwich. That's good. Perhaps the way to a man's heart really is through his stomach. Karl swallows his food, eyes narrowed in Erin's direction. She's never seen such a steely expression on his face before.

"I've been meaning to ask you, Ellie."

"Erin."

Karl blinks. "I'm sorry?"

"My name is Erin," Erin says. "I admit that I suspected you were a fairy when I gave you that false name."

Karl raises a brow. "Well, I'm not very sure what that means, but... you've decided to grace me with your real name now?"

"Yes." Erin scrunches her face up, trying to keep from spitting the fruit punch out. When she finally swallows it, she asks, "What did you want to ask?"

"Well..." Karl folds his arms. "About the King's assault on Cassia..."

"What about it?"

"You said that they were after you and that we needed to leave immediately, and because of that..." Karl trails off. "Why did they attack? Why are they looking for you?"

Erin watches Karl carefully. He leans forward, fingers clenched into fists against the table; he is the very picture of a distraught man, desperate for answers that only she holds. Glee trickles through her veins, and Erin can hardly resist a grin spreading across her face.

"Well," Erin says, biting the insides of her cheeks to calm her expression. "I never told anyone this, but I'm the King's daughter."

Karl's eyes bulge from their sockets. "The King's daughter?"

Erin nods. How fun it is to see the abject shock on Karl's face.

"Then..." Karl wobbles his bottom lip between his teeth. "You're *actually* a princess? You escaped from the castle? You aren't from faraway lands?"

"Yes." Erin bows her head, feigning regret. If he becomes suspicious of her now, then her previous efforts would have been for naught. "I'm sorry for lying. I wasn't sure whether I could trust you, you know?"

Karl humphs. "Yeah, I get it. But why did you escape? I thought life in the castle was luxurious. You would have had everything you wanted."

Erin huffs. "How ignorant."

"What do you mean?"

"I was kept in a dungeon cell like an animal. No freedom, minimal food and water, and barely anything to do besides to read. I was constantly watched. All day, all night."

"I'm sorry."

"No, don't be." Erin peers up at him from under her lashes. "It's not your fault. It's my father's."

"Now he's coming after you and sending his entire legion of knights." Karl finishes the last of his sandwich and wipes his hands clean of crumbs.

"That's right. He wants me captured, no matter the cost. And he wants to make me a bride for the Prince of Aevum."

"That sucks."

"I prefer to be free. To make my own choices. I refuse to bend to his whims any longer."

Admiration sparkles in Karl's eyes. Erin's grin mirrors his.

"Well, I guess you're going to have to bring me along for the ride now," Karl says. "I've left Cassia behind—there's no-one left for me there."

"And besides, the knights are there."

"Yeah, they are."

"We can make a new life for ourselves in Astra." Erin sighs, a dreamy smile on her face as she stares out of the window, at the mountains in the distance. Small settlements dot the hills beside flowing streams, peeking out of forests. A strange building stands in the distance, its tip almost reaching the clouds. If Erin squints, she can just barely make out a clock's face.

"What is that?" Erin asks, gesturing at the tower.

Karl glances over. "That's Astra's clock tower. A defining feature, really."

"Are we approaching Astra? We've been travelling a long time."

"It's the final stop."

Erin sinks back into her seat and crosses her arms.

Karl glances over at her empty glass. "Are you done eating?"

"Yes."

"Shall we go, then?"

"Can we explore the train?" Erin asks. "It has so many facilities in one place. I wonder if it would have a carriage with a better view."

"A better view? Of what?"

"The scenery. Is it not relaxing to simply sit and stare out at the pastures all day?" Erin asks. "I do love myself some adventure from time to time, but it's good if we stopped to smell the roses sometimes."

"Well then." Karl rises from his seat. "Let's go find that carriage of yours."

Erin lifts her head at that suggestion. She removes herself from the booth and bounds towards the other end of the dining car.

"Wait! Ell—Erin! We haven't paid yet!"

# Chapter 6

## Train Wreck

The viewing car, at the very end of the train, is fitted with white picnic tables and benches. The awning above their heads rustles noisily in the wind. The wooden floorboards tremble against their feet. But Erin does not mind—these things only add to the ambience. Karl twirls an arrow between his fingers, for lack of anything better to do.

The train pulls into a stop in the middle of a forest, the station crawling with weeds and rife with bugs. Ghostly passengers float up the steps, ectoplasmic luggage in tow. Erin watches from her seat, frowning.

"Why are they taking so long?"

"There are quite a few of them," Karl observes.

Once the final passenger boards, the train's whistle blows. The train departs once more; hissing steam erupts from between its wheels.

Erin perks her ears up. There was another sound separate from the train's groans. A sense of foreboding washes over her like the chill of a snowy draft. She snaps her head towards the foreign rumble, only to catch sight of a locomotive barrelling towards them, showing no signs of stopping.

"Look out!"

Erin grabs Karl's arm and drags him away from the seat. A terrified scream rings out in the air. Erin and Karl are knocked to the ground, debris skimming over their crouched bodies. Erin lifts her head to see a fairy pierced through the chest with jagged shrapnel. Another guest lies beneath a pile of rubble, a single unmoving arm sticking out, bent at the wrong angle.

Erin grits her teeth. "This is bad."

Emblazoned with the emblem of the kingdom—the emblem of the *King*—the offending train keeps charging forward, driving its crumpled engine against the Midnight Express.

Erin hops to her feet, pulling Karl up with her. She drags him away from the scene of destruction and onto the next carriage.

"W-Where are we going?" Karl shouts over the shrieks and screams behind them.

Erin kicks the door open, finding the service robots waving their arms and directing the guests to the front carriages. The Express rattles on the rails, carriages shunting to the side. Erin hits the wall with a painful thud.

A door slams, the bang resonating in Erin's ears. Erin's eyes widen, reacting instinctively, and shoves herself and Karl to the carpet, out of the reach of the gnarly finger bursting through the door. It gropes around searchingly. Failing to find them, it withdraws, replaced by a crimson eye amidst wispy fogs of shadow.

Erin wastes no time in picking herself up and bolts past the throngs of robots helping guests, both healthy and injured. She shoves them aside and rushes over to the next car.

A crowd gathers at the entrance of the dining car, clambering and crawling over one another through the too-narrow doorway. One elf rips a fairy's wings and tosses the screeching creature aside. The bloodied remains of a stamped-out gnome lies on the ground, pummelled by hooves and shoes alike.

"Please remain calm!" an automated female voice calls from the other car. "We will open—"

Erin snarls. She *has* to get to the next car, no matter what. She cannot risk—

The ceiling shatters, raining dust and rubble upon them. Karl winds an arm around Erin's waist and the duo falls against the wall. They barely dodged the sweep of a massive hand. It snatches a satyr up, the helpless creature writhing and screaming as he is lifted out of the train.

The frantic yells of a manic crowd nearly drown out the crack of the satyr's bones. His fearful scream fades into the distance as he is, without a doubt, hurled away.

Another fairy is snatched, then a ghoul, then a pixie. Erin scarcely dares to breathe as the passengers are picked off one by one. Please let it not be her. *Please.*

As the crowd thins out, the doorway becomes clear once again. As soon as the arm retracts from the hole, Erin and Karl dive through it to the next carriage.

The dining car is all smashed up, the floor littered with cracked porcelain plates and shards of glass. Tables are overturned, chairs fallen on their sides, creating a winding maze that weaves and threads through the sundered carriage cart. Erin steps over the spilled food, and the piles of shattered cutlery. Acutely aware of the sudden chitters and squeals coming up from behind them.

"Goblins!" Karl shouts. "There are goblins behind us!"

Erin shoots a look at the open door leading into the next set of cabin cars, the deluxe suites. Something whizzes by her head, whisking through her hair and stabbing into the wall in front of them. A crossbow bolt!

Several robots storm in from the next carriage, rolling by on caterpillar wheels, their determined, digital expressions displayed on their monitors. Erin narrows her eyes. She still has the dagger in her boots—she will not let them get in the way.

"Dear guests! Please make your way to the front of the train!" the robots chant. Erin recognizes two of the robots—Belle and Brendan. "We will protect you!"

As absurd as that statement sounds, Erin pushes her derision aside. Right now, any distraction is a good distraction. Erin scrambles past the door, jostling between the robots, with Karl directly behind her.

Shots ring out from the robots' own arsenal of weaponry. The goblins' throaty cries fill the air, slain by the robots' bullets. Too fast to dodge, so powerful that they tear through the goblins. Blood splatters to the ground, practically invisible against the crimson carpet.

Erin chances a glance back, seeing a legion of goblins hurtling through to the dining car. Their numbers grow by the second. There is no way the robots can keep up with the onslaught for much longer.

"Distinguished guests, please—"

Belle swivels its head on its neck, its monitor splintered, full of bolts and shrapnel and cracked beyond recognition. Its voice is horribly distorted, painful to listen to. "Please hu-hu-hurry to the front-front-front—."

Erin grasps the lever by the doorway, her fingers curled tightly around its knobbly handle.

It's now or never. With a heave, she pulls.

"Erin? What are you doing?" Alarmed, Karl grabs her arm, yanking her away from the lever.

However, he is too late. The train's carriages separate. Their carriage zooms away from the ones the robots and the goblins are battling it out on.

"M-Miss?"

The rattle of wheels against tracks soon drowns out Belle's weak voice. Erin merely watches as the carriage, infested with goblins and knights, is left behind. The threat is over now. They are safe.

"Why did you do that?" Karl grabs Erin's shoulder and shakes her. "There were people still on the carriage. Why did you—"

"I did it for our safety." Erin shrugs Karl's hands off. "I did it so we could survive, Karl."

*Why does he not understand?*

"But we..." Karl trails off. Erin spies something in his eyes, something dark. Something *fearful*.

Like a prey animal.

How... interesting. And how delightful.

"The threat has been neutralized," she says. "Let's go and find somewhere to watch the fields go by. That will calm your nerves, I'm sure. Maybe we can have some tea while we're at it."

Erin hums a happy tune as she strides off towards the end of the carriage. There must be another viewing platform somewhere on the train or another dining car with long windows.

Erin's stomach grumbles. It *has* been a while since they ate those sandwiches. It's high time they get something else to eat. With that insufferable serving robot— what was its name again? Brandon? —permanently gone, they could order as much food as they'd like.

It takes her a few seconds to realize that Karl is not following. Turning back, she finds Karl still standing at the other end of the carriage. The carriages they left behind are already out of view as what remains of the Express swerves around the mountain. His back is to her, hair golden in the sun, his locks tousled messily in the howling wind.

They appear incredibly soft. Perhaps Erin should run her fingers through them once in a while. It *could* be calming.

"Are you coming?" she calls.

Karl slowly turns, Adam's Apple bobbing. He answers quietly and plods over to her.

"I'm starving. Let's find some food." Erin glances out the window. The city of Astra is not far now, its alien buildings shimmering in the afternoon rays. Soon, they will reach their destination, a place to start her life anew.

Her life of freedom.

# Chapter 7

## Astra

Astra is larger than the castle, larger still than the town of Cassia. Skyscrapers reach for the skies, carrying with them billboards of glitzy colours, advertising products Erin had never seen before. The streets are paved with smooth concrete and the roads, with asphalt. Thin trees flank the path, wooden benches circling their roots.

All manner of creatures populate the broad streets, living their own little lives. Doing their own little thing. Having exciting conversations, sprinting with all their might to catch the trams, gushing at the displays of clothes collated in shop windows.

"What's that, Karl?" Erin asks, gesturing to a stand with a long queue. People walk away from it with a white swirl in a cup, soaked in liquids of different consistencies and colours.

"It's..." Karl mumbles absently. He looks down at the map in his hands, something he took from the station. "That's ice cream."

"Can we get some?"

"We don't have any money right now, Erin. I left most of my savings in the pack."

"We could just ask very politely." Faux courtesy got her very far in her life in the castle. Ask nicely for extra meat, and the goblins would give it to her without a second thought.

"That won't work here."

Erin pouts. "Never try, never know."

"Erin, we have to find accommodation for the night. Somewhere affordable where we can stay."

"Affordable?"

"We need to pay for our rooms." Met with Erin's blank expression, Karl pinches his fingers—that same cryptic gesture from before—and rubs them together in very much the same way. "Money."

Erin claps her hands, a bright smile on her face. She remembers money. Ka-ching, it went. "You mean like how we paid for food and our train tickets?"

"Yeah."

"A bed sounds nice, too. Maybe when we get ourselves settled, we can come back out and explore. There are just so many new things to see!"

Karl has a funny look in his eyes as he returns his focus to the map. "I guess... we could."

"Lead the way." Erin makes a sweeping gesture, almost knocking into an elderly lady with her waving hand. She ignores the piercing glare shot back at her.

Karl sighs and sets off down a side street towards the suburban areas. Erin traipses behind him, curious as to what kind of lodgings he would be able to get them.

"WELL, I WAS HOPING we'd get somewhere better, but Astra only offers rooms for sky-high prices."

His words are akin to the buzz of a bug in Erin's ears as she throws open the door to their motel room. It is somewhat cramped, a couple of insects scuttling about on the floor, but it provides an excellent view of the cityscape.

Erin approaches the balcony and squashes a roach under her foot. "It's fantastic."

"Really?"

Erin stands in the gentle embrace of the wind, taking in the sights and sounds of Astra: a city that wows her with every step she takes, and every scent she smells. It is so different from the castle, so different from the sleepy town of Cassia Springs.

So...

Freeing.

"Karl, come and look! It's beautiful."

Karl plods over, his footsteps silent on the fluffy carpet. He joins her on the balcony, leaning against the railing.

"We should go there sometime." Erin gestures at the clock tower in the middle of the city, lit up and sparkling in the dark of night. The one they saw all the way from the mountain pass, back on the Midnight Express. Perhaps she could make it her home one day. Who wouldn't want to live in a shining beacon?

"Maybe tomorrow. I need to make arrangements to go back to Cassia."

"Cassia? Why?" Erin shakes her head. "You said we can stay in Astra. You promised!"

"I know." Karl runs a hand through his hair. "I thought about it, and I realized... we don't have anything out here, Erin. No money, no contacts... no-one. We won't be able to survive for long."

"We could just sleep in the clock tower and take food from people."

"That's—"

Karl opens his mouth to rebut, only to be silenced with a firm press of her lips on his. He lets out a surprised squeak that Erin swallows whole. Her fingers curl into his hair, the other hand tugging insistently on his arm.

Karl tears himself away from her. Erin tilts her head, peering into his dark eyes. All she sees is a scared animal, unsure as to whether he should run or hide.

A surge of power courses through her veins. Like how King Arthur must have felt when he pulled the Excalibur from the stone.

"Why did you do that?" Karl asks, breathless.

"Because you were talking way too much. Perish those thoughts. We're never going back to Cassia. The train's a wreck, and it's too far to walk. We'd die from starvation or fall to the elements before we could even get halfway back."

"That's…"

Karl falters. He searches for an argument but finds none. He drops his eyes to the ground, his shoulders slumped.

"Great," Erin finishes for him. She grins. "We'll sleep at the clock tower and stargaze every night."

"What about our food situation? I could find a job, but—"

"What's a job?"

Karl coughs. "Work. We do something for other people, and they'll pay us money."

"That sounds like a lot of effort for such low returns."

"We have to survive somehow, Erin. We can't just fool around all day."

"I don't see why not. There's plenty of food around here. We can just grab some and eat under the tower."

Karl blanches. "But that's *stealing*!"

"It's stealing if we get caught. If we do…" Erin smiles. She reaches for the knife in her boot and holds it up for Karl to see. The blade glints in the light. Karl takes a step back, not bothering to conceal the shock on his face. Shock or horror, she does not know.

"This is going right into the heart of anyone who tries to stop us."

"But—"

"If you don't want any part of this, you could head on home. I'm not stopping you. But Mel isn't there anymore." Erin hums. "Or you could go live with Susan! I'm sure she'd welcome you back with open arms!"

Karl bites his lip, turning to the balcony's edge.

"We should sleep now," Erin declares. "Tomorrow, we're going to be doing a lot of sight-seeing."

Karl does not budge. Erin frowns. He will come to his senses soon. She just needs to be patient.

Erin throws herself onto the bed, shooing flies from under the covers. She snuggles into a tattered pillow, ignoring the strong musky stench of the sheets. At this point, nothing can deter her excitement, not when the scent of adventure beckons her.

She cracks open an eye as Karl joins her on the bed, crawling under the covers and burying himself beneath the quilt. Erin listens to the faint mutterings under his breath, watching the way his chest falls and rises.

It is only when she is certain that he is asleep does she let herself drift off. After all, who knows what Karl could do to her when she's utterly defenceless?

# Chapter 8

## The Clocktower

For breakfast the next day, they tuck into cream buns stolen from a quaint little bakery next to the motel. Erin swiped them off the shelves, sticky fingers grabbing two and shoving under her tunic as Karl keeps watch. The gnome on the other end of the counter didn't suspect a thing; she was busy ringing up another customer's purchase, after all. Heist successful, they step out onto the lively streets of Astra.

Karl nibbles his bread, while Erin chomps heartily on hers. The cream bun is delicious, the sugary gloop bursting in her mouth in the first bite. If all their bread is this good, then Erin may have to consider paying this bakery a visit again sometime.

At Erin's request, Karl takes her to the clocktower. Its white columns gleam in the morning sun. Erin squints, the glare of the reflection stabbing at her eyes. Nature's rude assault aside, Erin is content. Listening to the staccato ticks of the minute hand, whiling leisurely under the grandest timepiece Erin has ever seen in her life, it all has a touch of magic that no other place could ever offer.

"How's the bread?" Erin asks. She has long since finished her share. Karl licks cream off his thumb.

"It's good."

Erin smiles. "We should go back and get more next time."

"Legally. We'll get them legally."

Erin wants to scoff. Karl and his integrity. Does he not realize? Integrity's a prison, and she'll be damned if she lets herself be caged again after such a bitter battle for her freedom.

One day, he will come around. She will make sure of that.

Erin pauses at a shadow in the skies, tensing at the whip of the sudden gales. She squints, her brows furrowed at the massive creature circling overhead, blocking out the sun. She can recognize that demonic form anywhere. It weaves through the clouds, wings spread, each beat bringing blustering gusts of wind that rock the buildings and trees. The dragon soars over the city, crimson scales glinting menacingly in the light of the sun. Its bellow can be heard for miles, echoing through every street and every corner of Astra, and even the rolling hills beyond.

Erin grits her teeth, grasping at Karl's wrist. Karl nearly drops his bread, his mouth agape. There is only one thought in Erin's mind.

There is no escape.

The dragon—the *Dragon-King*—roars as he flies over the clocktower, smoke streaming from his nostrils and fire, from his mouth. Plunged into pandemonium, citizens flee, scrambling to get far, far away. Trees quiver violently in storms as strong as tempests. Erin throws an arm up to shield herself, her knees bent and body close to the ground, fighting against the wind.

"Erin! Quick, we have to go!" Karl tugs at her arm, but Erin wrenches it away. She keeps her head angled to the sky, at the horrifying sight of her father landing upon the tower, spitting jets of fire at hapless citizens. His large, golden eyes peek from between the hides of his scales and peers down at her, as though staring into Erin's soul.

"I found you at last, my *dear* daughter," the King bellows. "Return to the castle, and I shall harm no-one in this *fair* town."

Erin reaches for her weapon, her only defence against this dragon—the dagger in her boot. Against a dragon at least ten times her height, a hundred times her bulk, a measly dagger wouldn't even scratch his scales.

But she has to face him down—right here, right now—or she will never, ever be free. Not when her father can pursue her to the edges of the earth. Not when his very existence threatens the freedom she worked so hard to gain.

She cannot let him take her or her efforts would have been in vain.

"I will not, Father!" Erin calls, unsure if her voice could even reach him. She stands with her back straight, ignoring her hair tossed about by the wind. "I will not bow down to you any longer!"

Karl grabs her shoulder, but she shrugs his hand away without even sparing him a glance. "Erin, you can't possibly *hope* to—"

"Do you dare defy me?" The King laughs, his mocking cackle reverberating throughout the field.

Erin says nothing. He doesn't deserve a response. Not after all that he has done to her.

"In that case," the King bellows, "I will have to take you by force!"

"You may certainly try," Erin whispers. Too quiet for anyone to hear, even Karl. The dragon swoops from his perch, a deafening roar splitting Erin's eardrums. Claw outstretched, he makes a grab for Erin. She shoves Karl aside and rolls out of the way. She stumbles to her feet, lifting her head and gazing towards where the dragon takes to the skies once more.

She has to get to higher ground. It's the only way to fight against an opponent who can fly.

"Erin!" Karl cries. "Where are you going?"

Erin tears towards the tower, to the staircase that would take her to the observation deck. From there, she will finally be on equal footing with her father. No longer a mite bending to his every whim, with no control over her own life.

It is time to settle this once and for all.

The journey to the top is tough, leaving her no time to rest. Debris rains from the ceiling, forcing her to keep moving or else she will be buried by the rubble. At a particularly violent tremor, Erin yelps, her body launched forward and onto the stairs.

She winces as pain shoots through her shin. The stairs crumble with every whack of the dragon's tail against the walls, dust swirling around her like clouds of mist. Erin picks herself up, flinching at the pain rattling her bones.

She cannot stop now. She has to make it to the very top. She *has* to.

Erin pulls herself up the final steps, emerging triumphantly onto the empty observation deck with its large windows and magnificent view of Astra's skyline. The rhythmic clunk of its clockwork rings in Erin's ears. She grasps her knees, struggling to catch her breath, battling the rising bile bitter on her tongue.

Erin lifts her head at a shadow cast upon her. A golden eye stares down at her, triumph dancing in that malicious glow. A claw crashes through the glass, shattering it. Thrusting upon her an explosion of shards, glaring iridescently in the sunlight.

Throwing her arms up in defence, she lunges to one side. She grimaces at the scratches dashed across her skin. Blood oozes from deeper cuts, trickling down her skin as she staggers to her feet. The claw cuts the air with a wide sweep, and fear courses through Erin's body when those gnarled claws lashes around her waist.

"Cease!" the King roars.

His grip is tight, so tight it almost snaps her ribs. Erin kicks and struggles. A strangled scream tears from her throat, the King dragging her from the deck and out into the open skies.

The air is thin here, much too thin for her to breathe. Erin gasps, grasping her throat as she struggles to fill her starved lungs with air. The dragon coos, brandishing its razor fangs.

"We shall return, you and I. And I will not allow for this insol—"

"Erin!"

Her eyes dart to a familiar voice. Karl stands on the observation deck, bow in hand and arrow nocked. The dragon's mocking laugh echoes in Erin's ears. But Erin merely smiles.

"Let her go!" Karl shouts.

"Who are you to come between me and my daughter?" the King taunts. "Naught but a midget."

Erin tightens her grip on her knife. Her father's guard is down. He thinks he's won.

Without hesitation, she plunges her blade deep into the King's claw. It slides past his scales, digging deep into dragon flesh. The King bellows in agony, his grip loosened, barely but enough for Erin to wriggle from his grasp. She clings to his arm, gripping so tight her fingers hurt, lest she plunges to the ground.

In the same moment, Karl lets his arrow fly, aim straight and true. The arrow pierces the King's eye, and blood spurts from the wound like a firework. Just one of those magnificent festival fireworks from Cassia Springs.

The King roars, his claws reaching up to scrabble at the wound, taking Erin with them. She seizes the chance, throwing herself forward, landing harshly on the dragon's rough back.

The dragon convulses, his body rumbling with each pained cry. Erin's fingers sting, slicing her hands on the sheer sharpness of his scales as she desperately clings to his reptilian flesh. She stuffs the grip of the knife into her mouth and begins to climb, one painstaking scale after another...

The dragon's wingbeats grow frantic as the two descend. Erin keeps her head low, her body close, as she crawls up his neck. If she can reach his eye, she can plunge her knife into that thick skull of his and—

Claws rip through trees, knocking branches and leaves down from their canopies. Already, Erin can see machines of flight hovering over them, choppers churning in the air. Are those...?

The Defence Force? Have they come to apprehend her father?

*That's...*

Erin grits her teeth, bracing herself as the dragon crashes to the ground.

*She cannot allow them to.*

Erin runs up his neck, almost tripping as the dragon writhes. She reaches his head and holds the knife up high, blade glinting in the light.

"N-No! Erin! My daughter! What are you—"

*She must kill her father with her own two hands.*

Without a word, Erin plunges the knife into the dragon's head, twisting and turning as she cracks into bone. The dragon roars, claws batting at her. But they are clumsy, and she is small. Erin dodges his swipes easily—he is no challenge compared to the knights and the goblins with crossbows.

His flailing arms weaken, and his struggles start to cease. Erin stands, wiping her hands clean of gushing red blood. She wrenches the knife from the dragon's head, slick with brain matter and dripping crimson. The dragon's glassy eyes remain open, staring into nothingness.

Dark clouds gather overhead. Lightning forks through the sky, and thunderclaps roll for miles. The fresh smell of rain permeates the air. Very soon, a revitalising downpour will lash down upon them.

She did it. She is now free, in all senses of the word. Her father is gone for good; there is no-one to send guards after her anymore. No-one to take her back to her cell in the castle.

At last, she is truly free, and no-one can stop her now.

# Epilogue

"**E**rin!"

Erin turns at the sound of her name, glancing over at the man rushing out from the staircase of the clocktower. The police are already here, the sirens from their cars blaring in her ears. She shoves the knife into her boot where it rightfully belongs.

"Erin, you..."

Karl grimaces, a hand covering his mouth as he stares at the sight in front of him.

Rain begins to fall. Heavy droplets descend in sheets from the dark clouds above. The intermittent flashes of lightning only add to the atmosphere. It charges the sky like the energy in her muscles, sizzling up to her chest.

Erin steps off her father's corpse, leaving him bleeding out in the sodden streets of Glasgow. The rush of exhilaration, the sheer thrill, is unmatched. It sears through her veins, giving her strength she never knew she had.

"Erin, we have to go." Karl grabs her wrist. "Come on! Before the cops get us!"

Erin agrees. No way is she going back to a jail cell after all she has done to get free.

The clock chimes above them, tolls ringing throughout the city. Karl takes the lead, darting down the concrete path and keeping his head down, dragging Erin along with him. Erin hopes he knows where he's going, and she sure hopes that he is not delivering them to the constables.

They skitter down an alleyway, away from the prying eyes of the public. The darkness of the shade consumes them, even in the middle of the day. Karl presses his back flush against the brick wall, panting loud and shuddering.

"Why the hell did you do that?" Karl hisses. "You didn't have to-... you didn't have to kill him!"

"He was threatening my freedom," she snarls. "Don't question me on things you don't understand."

"I *want* to understand, Erin!" Karl grasps her shoulders tightly, stopping just short of shaking her. "Why did you do these things? Why did you leave Mel to die? Why did you leave those people to die on the train? Why did you kill your own father...?"

Erin glares at him. Karl staggers back. The fear on his face is stark: the furrowed brows; narrowed eyes; and the parted lips. Unable to comprehend. Unable to understand.

No-one will be able to understand.

"They weren't people, Karl. They were robots. And my father's a tyrant. No-one cares if they live or die."

"What do you mean? What robots? What dragon?"

Erin can hardly recall their faces. Mel was a crass dwarf who sold knives and machetes in a town a short ride from the capital. Belle was a kindly woman who spoke with a gentle lilt. Brendan was a hearty man who served them dutifully.

And that is all she remembers of them.

They're not worth remembering.

Erin lifts her head at the sound of the shrill sirens. They have to go soon—no doubt the police are looking for them. She turns to Karl, who holds a hand to his temple, caught in internal conflict.

"We have to go." Erin touches his arm, and Karl flinches. He looks up at her, uncertainty dancing in his eyes.

She knows nothing about the outside world. She had been locked in the basement for all her life. All thanks to her father. Without Karl's help, she...

"I need you, Karl," Erin whispers, laying her palm flat on his chest. His breathing hitches; his heart thunders in his ribcage. Fluttering, nervous and afraid. "I can't live without you."

Karl presses his lips into a thin line but does nothing to stop her when she yanks him down the alleyway, past druggies shooting up, and unsavoury characters hanging out in dingy cafés.

Their adventure is only just beginning, but it's going to get a lot better. An adventure fit for a free girl.

Erin can feel it in her bones.

# About the Author

Enyale explores worlds with her mind, and transforms them into words on the page. Be it fantasy lands of Luminaries and deities, or houses with skeletons in their closets. When she's not writing, Enyale is either curled up with a thriller, or keeping her thumbs busy with the newest video game.